The Red Cross Girls in the British Trenches

CW00858748

The Red Cross Girls in the British Trenches

Margaret Vandercook

Vij Books India Pvt Ltd
New Delhi (India)

Published by

Vij Books India Pvt Ltd
(Publishers, Distributors & Importers)
2/19, Ansari Road
Delhi – 110 002
Phones: 91-11-43596460, 91-11-47340674
Mobile: 98110 94883
e-mail: contact@vijpublishing.com
www.vijbooks.in

Copyright © 2022,

ISBN: 978-93-93499-43-1

Contents

CHAPTER I
A Social Failure

T he dance was over and Mildred Thornton climbed disconsolately up the long stairs. From her thin shoulders floated a delicate white scarf and her dress was of white lace and tulle. Yet Mildred had no look of a conquering Princess, nor yet of Cinderella, who must have carried her head proudly even after the ball, remembering the devotion of her Prince.

But for Mildred there was no Prince to remember, nor devotion from anyone. She was in that mood of hopeless depression which comes from having attended a dance at which one has been a hopeless failure. Her head drooped and though her cheeks were hot, her hands were cold.

Downstairs in the library she could hear her brother having his good-night talk with their mother. Of course he did not intend that she should overhear what was being said, and yet distinctly his words floated up to her.

"Well, dearest, I did what I could, I swear it. Do hand me another one of those sandwiches; playing the devoted brother takes it out of me. But poor old Mill is no go! The fellows were nice enough, of course; they danced with her whenever I asked them, but the worst of it was they would not repeat the offense. You know Mill dances something like an animated telegraph pole, and though she is a brick and all that, she hasn't an ounce of frivolous conversation. Do you know, I actually heard her talking about the war, and no one in our set ever speaks of the war now; we are jolly tired of the subject."

Whatever her mother's reply, it was given in so low a tone as to be inaudible. But again Dick's voice was pitched louder.

"Oh, all right, I'll keep up the struggle a while longer, as I promised, but it's no use. Have you ever thought of what will become of your adored son's popularity if he has to continue in New York society with a 'Mill' stone hung about his neck?"

On the stairs the girl bit her lips, flinging back her head to keep the tears away. For at once there had followed the sound of her brother's pleased laugh over his own wit, then her mother's murmured protest.

So plainly could Mildred Thornton see the picture in the library that it was not necessary for her to be present except in the spirit. Indeed, it was in order that she might not intrude upon Dick's confession that she had insisted upon going at once to her own room as soon as they arrived at home. Nevertheless, no one need tell her that her brother had not the faintest intention of being unkind. He never liked hurting people's feelings; yet when one is handsome and charming, sometimes it is difficult to understand how those who are neither must feel.

In her own room a moment later, Mildred, touching the electric button, flooded her apartment with a soft yellow light. Then deliberately placing herself before a long mirror the girl began a study of her own appearance. After all, was she so much less good looking than other girls? Was that the reason why Dick had been compelled to report to their mother her extraordinary lack of social success? And if this had been the only occasion, once would not have mattered. But after three months of the same story, with everything done to help her, beautiful clothes, her own limousine, her father's money and reputation, her mother's and brother's efforts—why, no wonder her family was discouraged. But if only her mother had not been so disappointed and so chagrined, Mildred felt she would not have cared a great deal. There were other things in life besides society.

Yet now, without fear or favor, Mildred Thornton undertook to form an impartial judgment of herself.

In the mirror she saw reflected a girl taller than most girls, but even in these days when slenderness is a mark of fashion, certainly one who was too thin. However, there was comfort in the fact that her shoulders were broad and flat and that she carried her head well.

"For one must find consolation in something," Mildred murmured aloud. Then because she did not consider that the consolations were as numerous as they might have been, she frowned. It was unfortunate, of course, that her hair, though long and heavy, was also straight and flaxen and without the yellow-brown lights that were so attractive. Then assuredly her chin was too square and her mouth too large.

Closer she peered into the mirror. Her nose was not so bad; it could not be called piquant, nor yet pure Greek, but it was a straight, American nose. And at any rate her eyes were fairly attractive; if one wished to be flattering they might even be called handsome. They were almost steel color, large and clear, with blue and gray lights in them. Her eyebrows and lashes were much darker than her hair. If only their expression had not always been so serious!

Turning her head first on one side and then on the other, attempting to dart ardent, challenging glances at herself, suddenly Mildred made a little grimace. Then throwing back her head she laughed. Instantly the attraction she had been hoping for appeared in her face although the girl herself was not aware of it.

"Mildred Thornton, what an utter goose you are! It is tragic enough to be a stick and a wall flower. But when you attempt behaving like the girls who are belles, you simply look mad."

Moving aside from the mirror Mildred now let her party gown slip to the floor.

She was standing in the center of a beautiful room whose walls were gray and gold. The rug under her feet was also gray with a deep border of yellow roses. Her bed was of mahogany and there was a mahogany writing desk and table and low chairs of the same material. Through an open door one could glimpse a private sitting room even more charming. Indeed, as there was no possible luxury missing so there could be no doubt that Mildred Thornton was a fortunately wealthy girl, which of course meant that she had nothing to trouble her.

Nevertheless, at this moment Mildred was thinking, "Oh, if only I were thirty instead of nineteen, I wonder if I might be allowed to be happy in my own way."

Then without remembering to throw a dressing gown across her shoulders, tip-toeing across the floor without any apparent reason, the girl unlocked a secret drawer in her desk. Opening it she drew out a large, unusual looking envelope. She was staring at this while her eyes were slowly filling with tears, when there came a sudden knock at her door.

At the same instant the envelope was thrust back into the drawer, and not until then did Mildred answer or move toward her door.

A visit from her mother tonight was really one of the last things in the world she desired. It was wicked to have so little sympathy with one's own mother and the fault was of course hers. But tonight she was really too tired and depressed to explain why she had made no more effort to be agreeable. Her mother would insist that she had only herself to blame for her evening's failure. It was hard, of course, that so beautiful a woman could not have had a handsome daughter as well as a handsome son.

But instead of her mother, there in the hall stood a tall, thin man, whose light hair had turned gray. He had a strong, powerful face, deeply lined, one that both men and women turned to look at the second time.

"I heard you come upstairs alone, Mill dear," Judge Thornton said, smiling like a shamefaced schoolboy. "Don't tell your mother or Dick, will you, for we had better break it to them by degrees? But I sent a check today for two thousand dollars to the Red Cross Fund to be used in this war relief business, my dear. I had to do it, it was on my conscience. I know your mother and brother won't like it; they have been scolding for a new motor car and I've said I couldn't afford one. Really four persons ought to be able to get on with two automobiles, when a good many thousands are going without bread. We'll stand together, won't we, even if my little girl has to give up one of her debutante parties?"

Already Mildred's arms were about her father's neck so that he found it difficult to talk, for that and other reasons.

"I am so glad, so glad," she kept whispering. "You know how tiresome Dick and mother feel I am because I don't think we ought to keep on playing and dancing and frivoling, when this horrible war is going on and people are being wounded and killed every minute. If you only guessed how I wanted to use the little knowledge and strength I have to help."

But the Judge now shook his head decisively and moved away.

"Nonsense, child, you are too young; such an idea is not to be thought of. We ought never to have let you attend those hospital classes, or at least I should not have allowed it. Goodness knows, your mother fought the idea bitterly enough! But remember, you promised her that you would give the same time to society that you have given to your nursing, and that is three years. You can't go back on your word, and besides I won't have you thinking so much about these horrors; you'll be making yourself ill. War isn't a girl's business." Certainly Judge Thornton was trying to be severe, but just beyond the door he turned back.

"I sent the check in your name, Mill dear, so you can feel you are doing a little something to help," he added affectionately. "Good night."

Afterwards, although tired (and it was quite two o'clock when she was finally in bed), Mildred Thornton found it almost impossible to sleep. At first she kept seeing a vision of herself as she appeared at the dance earlier in the evening. How stiff and solemn and out of place she had seemed, and how impossible it had been to make conversation with the young men her brother had brought forward and introduced to her! In the first place, they had not seemed like men at all, but like the fashionably dressed pictures in the magazine advertisements or the faultless figures adorning the windows in men's furnishing stores.

Besides, they had only wished to talk of the latest steps in the new dances or the last musical comedy. And what a strange expression that young fellow's face had worn, when she had asked him if he had ever thought of going over to help in the war! No wonder Dick had been so ashamed of her.

Then, having fallen asleep, Mildred began dreaming. Her father had been right, she must have been thinking more than she should about the war.

Because in her dream she kept seeing regiment after regiment of soldiers marching across broad, green fields, with bands playing, flags flying and their faces shining in the sun. Finally they disappeared in a cloud of black smoke, and when this took place she had awakened unexpectedly.

Sitting up in bed with her long flaxen braids hanging over either shoulder, Mildred wondered what had aroused her at this strange hour? Then she remembered that it was the loud, clear ringing of their front door bell. Moreover, she had since become conscious of other noises in the house. Her brother had rushed out of his room and was calling to the man servant who had turned on the lights down in the front hall.

"I say, Brown, be careful about opening that front door, will you? Wait half a moment until I get hold of my pistol and I'll join you. I don't like this business of our being aroused at a time like this. It must be just before daylight and New York is full of burglars and cutthroats."

Dick then retired into his room and the next sound Mildred heard was his voice expostulating with his mother.

"Oh, go on back to bed, dearest, and for heaven's sake keep father out of this. Certainly there is no danger; besides, if there were I am not such a mollycoddle that I'm going to have Brown bear the brunt. Somebody's got to open the door or that bell will never stop ringing."

Then Dick's feet in his bedroom slippers could be heard running down the uncarpeted stairs. A moment later Mildred got into her wrapper and stood with her arm about her mother's waist, shivering and staring down into the hall.

If anything should happen to Dick it would be too tragic! Her mother adored him.

The butler was now unfastening the storm doors, while directly behind him Dick waited with his pistol at a convenient level.

Then both men stepped backward with astonished exclamations, allowing a queer, small figure to enter the hall without a word of protest. The next moment Mildred was straining her ears to hear one of the most bewitching voices she had ever imagined. Later an equally bewitching figure unfolded itself from a heavy coat.

"It's sorry I am to have disturbed you at such an hour," the girl began. "But how was I to know that the train from Chicago would arrive at three o'clock in the morning instead of three in the afternoon? I was hoping some one would be at the station to meet me, though of course I didn't expect it, so I just took a cab and found the way here myself."

Then the newcomer smiled with a kind of embarrassed wistfulness.

For the first time beholding Dick's pistol, which was now hanging in a dangerously limp fashion in his hand, she started.

"Oh," she exclaimed, "I suppose you think that in Nebraska we go about with pistols in our hands instead of pocket handkerchiefs; but, really, we don't welcome guests with them."

Having dropped her coat on the floor, the girl under the light looked so tiny that she seemed like a child. She had short, curly dark hair which her tight-fitting traveling cap had pressed close against her face. Her eyes were big and blue, and perhaps because she was pale from fatigue her lips were extremely red.

Indeed, Dick Thornton decided, and never afterwards changed his opinion, that she was one of the best looking girls he had ever seen in his life. But who could she be, where had she come from, and what was she doing in their house at such an extraordinary hour?

Clearing his throat, Dick made a tremendous effort to appear impressive. Yet he was frightfully conscious of his own absurdity. He knew that his hair must be standing on end, that his dressing gown had been donned in a hurry and that he had on slippers with a space between his feet and dressing gown devoid of covering. Moreover, what was he to do with his absurd pistol?

"I am afraid you have made a mistake," Dick began lamely. "If you are a stranger in New York and have just arrived to visit friends, perhaps we can tell you where to find them. Or, or, if you—" Dick did not feel that it was exactly his place to invite a strange young woman to spend the rest of the night at their home; yet as her cab had gone one could hardly turn her out into the street. Why did not his mother or Mildred come on down and help him out. Usually he knew the right thing to say and do, but this situation was too much for him. Besides, the girl looked as if she might be going to cry.

But she was a plucky little thing, because instead of crying she tried to laugh.

"I have made a mistake, of course," she faltered. "I was looking for Judge Richard Thornton's home on Seventy-fourth Street, the number was 28 I thought. Has the cabman brought me to the wrong place?"

Slowly Mrs. Thornton was now approaching them with Mildred hovering in the background. But Dick did not altogether like the expression of his mother's face. It showed little welcome for the present intruder. Now what could he say to make her happier before any one else had a chance to speak.

"Why, that *is* my father's name and our address all right, and I expect we are delighted to see you. I wonder if you would mind telling us your name and where you have come from? You see, we were not exactly looking for a visitor, but we are just as glad to see you."

The girl had turned at once toward Mrs. Thornton and it was astonishing how much dignity she possessed in spite of her childish appearance.

"I regret this situation more than I can express. I am sure I owe you an explanation, although I do not know exactly what it can be," she began. "My name is Barbara Meade. Several weeks ago my father wrote to his old school friend, Judge Richard Thornton, saying that I was to be in New York for a short time on my way to England. He asked if it would be convenient to have me stay with you. He received an answer saying that it *would* be perfectly convenient and that I might come any day. Then before I left, father telegraphed." Barbara's lips were now trembling, although she still kept back the tears. "If you will call a cab for me, please, I shall be grateful to you. I would have gone to a hotel tonight, only I did not know whether a hotel would receive me at this hour."

"My dear child, you will do no such thing. There has been some mistake, of course, since I have never heard of your visit. But certainly we are not going to turn you out in the night," Mrs. Thornton interrupted kindly.

Ordinarily she was supposed to be a cold woman. Now her manner was so charming that her son and daughter desired to embrace her at the same moment. But there was no time for further discussion or demonstration, because at this instant a new figure joined the little group. Actually Judge Thornton looked more like a criminal than one of the most famous criminal lawyers in New York state.

Nevertheless, immediately he put his arm about Barbara Meade's shoulders.

"My dear little girl, you need never forgive me; I shall not forgive myself nor expect any one else to do so. Certainly I received that letter from your father. Daniel Meade is one of my dearest friends besides being one of the finest men in the United States. Moreover, I wrote him that we should be most happy to have his daughter stay with us as long as she liked, but the fact of the matter is—" several times the tall man cleared his throat. "Well, my family will tell you that I am the most absent-minded man on earth. I simply forgot to mention the matter to my wife or any one else. So now you have to stay on with us forever until you learn to forgive me."

Then Dick found himself envying his father as he patted their visitor's shoulder while continuing to beg her forgiveness.

But the next moment his mother and sister had led their little guest away upstairs. Then when she was safely out of sight Dick again became conscious of his own costume—or lack of it.

CHAPTER II
Different Kinds of Courage

M oving along Riverside Drive with sufficient slowness to grasp details had given the little western visitor an opportunity to enjoy the great sweep of the Hudson River and the beauty of the New Jersey palisades.

On the front seat of the motor car Barbara sat with Dick Thornton, who had offered to take the chauffeur's place for the afternoon. Back of them were Mrs. Thornton and Mildred. It was a cold April day and there were not many other cars along the Drive. Finally Mrs. Thornton, leaning over, touched her son on the shoulder.

"I think it might be wiser, Dick, to go back home now. Barbara has seen the view of the river and the wind has become so disagreeable. Suppose we turn off into Broadway," she suggested.

Acquiescing, a few moments later Dick swung his car up a steep incline. He was going at a moderate pace, and yet just before reaching Broadway he sounded his horn, not once, but half a dozen times. The crossing appeared free from danger. Then when they had arrived at about the middle of the street, suddenly (and it seemed as if the car must have leaped out of space) a yellow automobile came racing down Broadway at incredible speed.

It chanced that Barbara observed the car first, although immediately after she heard queer muffled cries coming from Mildred and her mother. She herself felt no inclination to scream. For one thing, there did not seem to be time. Nevertheless, impulse drew her eyes toward Dick Thornton to see how he was affected.

Of course he must have become aware of their danger when the rest of them had. He must know that all their lives were in deadly peril. Yet there was nothing in the expression of his face to suggest it, nor had his head moved the fraction of an inch. Strange to see him half smiling, his color vivid, his dark eyes unafraid, almost as if he had no realization of what must inevitably happen.

Closing her own eyes, Barbara felt her body stiffen; the first shock would be over in a second, and afterwards——

Nevertheless no horrible crash followed, but instead the girl felt that she must be flying along through the air instead of being driven along the earth.

For they had made a single gigantic leap forward. Then Barbara became aware that Mildred was speaking in a voice that shook with nervousness in spite of her effort at self-control.

"You have saved all our lives, Dick. How ever did you manage to get out of that predicament?" Afterwards she endeavored to quiet her mother, who was becoming hysterical now that they were entirely safe.

So they were safe! It scarcely seemed credible. Yet when Barbara Meade looked up the racing car was still speeding on its desperate way down Broadway, followed by two policemen on motorcycles, while their own automobile was moving quietly on. The girl had a moment of feeling limp and ill. Then she discovered that Dick Thornton was talking to her and that she must answer him.

He was still smiling and his brown eyes were untroubled, but now that the danger had passed every bit of the color had left his face. Yet undoubtedly he was good looking.

Barbara had to check an inclination to laugh. This was a tiresome trait of hers, to see the amusing side of things at the time when they should not appear amusing. Now, for instance, it was ridiculous to find herself admiring Dick Thornton's nose at the instant he had saved her life.

His face was almost perfectly modeled, his forehead broad and high with dark hair waving back from it like the pictures of young Greek boys. His brown eyes were deeply set beneath level brows, his olive skin and his mouth as attractive as a girl's.

Yes, her new acquaintance was handsome, Barbara concluded gravely, and yet his face lacked strength. Personally she preferred the bronzed and rugged type of young men to whom she was accustomed in the west.

But what was it that her companion had been saying?

"I do trust, Miss Meade, that you are not ill from fright. Mildred, will you please lend us mother's smelling salts for a little while, or had we best stop by a drug store?"

Shaking her head Barbara smiled. She was wearing the same little close-fitting brown velvet hat of the night of her arrival. But today her short curls had fluttered out from under it and her eyes were wide open and bluer than ever with the wonderful vision of the first great city she had ever seen.

"Oh, dear me, no, there is nothing in the world the matter with me," Barbara expostulated. "Why if I can't go through a little bit of excitement like that, how do you suppose I am going to manage to be a Red Cross nurse in Europe in war times?"

"You a war nurse?" Dick Thornton's voice expressed surprise, amusement, and disbelief. He turned his head sideways to glance at his companion. "Forgive me," he said, "but you look a good deal more like a bisque doll. I believe they do have dolls dressed as Red Cross nurses, set up in the windows of the toy shops. Shall I try to get a place in a window for you?"

Barbara was blushing furiously, although she intended not to allow herself to grow angry. Certainly she must not continue so sensitive about her youthful appearance. There would be many more trials of this same kind ahead of her.

"I am sorry you think I look like a doll," she returned with an effort at carelessness; "it is rather absurd in a grown-up woman to show so little character. My hair is short because I had typhoid fever a year ago. You know, I'm really over eighteen; I got through school pretty early and as I have always known what I wanted to do, I took some special courses in nursing at school, so I was able to graduate two years afterwards."

"Oh, I see," Dick murmured, appearing thoughtful. "Eighteen is older than any doll I ever heard of unless she happened to be a doll that had been put away in an old cedar chest years ago. Then she usually had the paint licked off, the saw-dust coming out and her hair uncurled." Again Dick glanced around, grave as the proverbial judge. "You know, it does not look to me as if any of those alarming things had *yet* happened to you, else I might try to turn doctor myself."

Good-naturedly Barbara laughed. If her new acquaintance insisted upon taking her as a joke, at least she had enough sporting blood not to grow angry, or at least if she were angry not to reveal it.

"Well, what *are* you going to be, Mr. Thornton?" Barbara queried, shrugging her shoulders the slightest bit. "As long as you need not develop into a physician on *my* account, are you to be a lawyer like your father?"

Dick suppressed a groan. To look at her would you ever have imagined that this little prairie flower of a girl would develop into a serious-minded young woman demanding to hear about "your career"? Any such idea must be nipped in the bud at once.

"Oh, no, I am certainly *not* going to study law, and if you don't mind my mentioning it, I get pretty bored with that suggestion. Everybody I meet thinks because my father is one of the biggest lawyers in the country that I must become his shadow. It is all right being known as my 'father's son' up to a certain point, but I'm not anxious to have comparisons made between us as lawyers."

Barbara felt uncomfortable. She had not intended opening a subject that seemed to be such an unfortunate one. So she only murmured, "I beg your pardon."

And though Dick laughed and answered, "Don't mention it," there was little more conversation between them for the rest of the drive home.

But once at home in the big, sunny library, stretched out in an arm chair, smoking while the girls were drinking tea, the young man became more amiable.

He had changed his outdoor clothes for a velvet smoking jacket and his shoes for a pair of luxurious pumps.

"I say, Mildred, old girl, would you mind ringing the bell and having Brown bring me some matches?" he asked. Finding his own gone, he had simply turned his head and smiled upon his sister. It happened that the bell was within only a few feet of him and she had to cross the room to accomplish his desire.

Although Mildred was tired from a strenuous half hour devoted to comforting her mother since their return from the ride, without protesting or even appearing surprised, she did as she was asked.

But Barbara Meade felt her own cheeks flushing. One need not stay in the Thornton household for four entire days, as she had, before becoming aware that it was the son of the family to whom every knee must bow. His mother, sister, the servants appeared to adore him. It was true that Judge Thornton attempted to show a little more consideration for his daughter, but he was so seldom at home and when there his attention was usually upon some problem of his own.

More than once Barbara had felt sorry for Mildred. Of course, her position looked like an enviable one as the only daughter of a wealthy and distinguished man, with a beautiful mother and a charming brother. Nevertheless, however little one liked to criticize their hostess even in one's own mind, Barbara could not but see that Mildred Thornton's life with her mother was a difficult one.

In the first place, Mrs. Thornton was a fashionable society woman. In spite of what might seem to most people riches, she was constantly talking about how extremely poor they were and how she hoped that Dick and Mildred would make matches that would bring money into the family. She had the same dark eyes and olive coloring that her son had inherited, and as her hair was a beautiful silver-white, it made her face appear younger. She seemed to treat her daughter Mildred's plainness as a personal insult to herself and behaved as though Mildred could have no feeling in the matter.

Several times the visitor had heard her refer to her daughter's lack of beauty before strangers.

But that Dick Thornton should dare treat his sister with the same lack of consideration was insufferable! Barbara had a short, straight little nose with the delicate nostrils that belong to most sensitive persons. Now she could not help their arching with disdain, although she hoped no one would notice her.

Yet Dick was perfectly aware of her indignation and amused by it. He was accustomed to having girls angry with him; it was one of the ways in which they showed their interest.

"I wonder if I would like to know what Miss Barbara Meade is at this moment thinking of me?" he demanded lazily, smiling from under his half-closed brown eyes and blowing a wreath of soft gray smoke into a halo about his own head.

The girl's blue eyes had the trick of darkening suddenly. It was in this way she betrayed her emotions before she could speak.

"I was thinking," she answered in a clear, cold little voice, "that I have always been sorry before I never had a brother. But now I am not so sure."

An abominably rude speech! The girl could not decide whether or not she regretted having made it. Certainly there was an uncomfortable silence in the big room until Mildred broke it.

She had been gazing thoughtfully into the fire, which the April day made agreeable, and talking very little. Now she shook her head in protest.

"Oh, brothers aren't altogether bad," she smiled.

Barbara stammered.

"No, of course not; I didn't mean that. You must both forgive me. You see, I have only a married sister who is years older than I am, and my father. I suppose I have gotten too used to saying whatever pops into my head. Perhaps the men in the west are more polite to girls than eastern men. I don't know exactly why, but they are bigger, stronger men; they live outdoors and because their lives are sometimes rough they try to have their manners gentle. Oh, goodness, I have said something else impolite, haven't I?" Barbara ended in such consternation that her host and hostess both laughed.

"Oh, don't mind me; please go right ahead if it relieves your feelings," Dick remarked so humorously that Barbara felt it might be difficult to dislike him intensely, however you might disapprove of him.

"Only," he added, "don't start shooting verbal fireworks at the poor wounded soldiers whom you are going to attempt to nurse. If a fellow is down and out they might prove fatal. I say, Mill, did you ever hear anything more absurd? Miss Meade has an idea that she is going over to nurse the British Tommies. She looks more like she needed a nurse herself—with a perambulator."

"Yes, I know, Barbara has talked it all over with me," Mildred replied. "We went together to the Red Cross headquarters today to see about arrangements, when she could cross and what luggage she should take with her. Four American girls are to go in a party and after they arrive in England they will be sent where they are most needed. You see, Barbara's mother was an Irish woman, so she feels she is partly British; and then her father was a West Point man. She meant to make her living as a nurse anyhow, so why shouldn't she be allowed to help in the war? I understand exactly how Barbara feels."

Still gazing into the fire, Mildred's face had grown paler and more determined. "You see, I am going with her. I offered my own services and was accepted this morning. We sail in ten days," she concluded.

"You, Mildred? What utter tommy-rot!" Dick exclaimed inelegantly. "The mater is apt to lock you up in your room on a bread-and-water diet for ten days for even suggesting such a thing." Then he ceased talking abruptly and pretended to be stifling a yawn. For, glancing up, he had discovered that his mother was unexpectedly standing in the doorway. She was dressed for dinner and looked very beautiful in a lavender satin gown, but the expression on her face was not cheering.

Evidently she had overheard Mildred's confession and his sister was in for at least a bad quarter of an hour. Personally Dick hoped his own words had not betrayed her. For although he was a fairly useless, good-for-nothing character, he wasn't a cad, and for some reason or other he particularly did not wish their visitor to consider him one.

CHAPTER III
Farewell

I n the same sitting room and in the same chair, half an hour later, sat Barbara Meade, but in a changed mood. She was alone.

More ridiculously childish than ever she looked, with her small face white and tears forcing their way into her eyes and down her cheeks.

Yet from the music room adjoining the library came such exquisite strains of a world-old and world-lovely melody sung in a charming tenor voice, that the girl was compelled to listen.

> "Drink to me only with thine eyes
> And I will pledge with mine."

Straight through the song went on to the end. But when it was finally finished there was a moment's silence. Then Dick Thornton appeared, standing between the portieres dividing the two rooms.

"Say, I am awfully sorry there was such a confounded row," he began. "But there is no use taking the matter so seriously, it is poor Mill's funeral, not yours. You seem to be the kind of independent young female who goes ahead and does whatever reckless thing she likes without asking anybody's advice. But I do wish you would give the scheme up too. Mildred will never be allowed to go with you. I don't approve of it any more than mother does. Just you stay on in New York and I'll show you the time of your life."

Dick looked so friendly and agreeable, enough to have softened almost any heart. But Barbara was still thinking of the past half hour.

"Thank you," she returned coldly. "I haven't the faintest idea of giving up my purpose, even to 'have the time of my life.' And I do think you were hateful not to have stood by your sister. Besides, you might at least have said that you did not believe I had tried to influence Mildred, when your mother accused me. She was extremely unkind."

Entering the library Dick now took a chair not far from their visitor's, so that he could plainly observe the expressions on her face.

"Of course, I didn't stand up for Mill; I wouldn't let her go into all that sorrow and danger, even if mother consented," he protested. "Your coming here and all the talk you two girls have had about the poor, brave, wounded soldiers and such stuff, of course has influenced Mill. It has even influenced me—a little. But the fact is the war in Europe isn't our job."

"No, perhaps not," the girl answered slowly, perhaps that she might add the greater effect; "but would you mind telling me just what is your job? You have already told me so many things that were not. Is it doing one-steps and fox trots and singing fairly well? I presume I don't understand New York society, for out west our young men, no matter how rich their fathers happen to be, try to amount to something themselves; they do *some* kind of work."

Under his nonchalant manner Dick had become angry. But no one knew better than he the value of appearing cool in a disagreement with a girl. So he only shrugged his shoulders in a dandified fashion.

"I wonder why you think I am not at present engaged in a frantic search for a job on which to expend my magnificent energy?" Here Dick purposely yawned, extending his long legs into a more reposeful position. "The fact is, I believe I must have been waiting for an uncommonly frank young person from the west to give me the benefit of her advice. What would you suggest as a career for me? Remember, I saved your life this afternoon, so you may devote it to the unfortunate. Now what would you think of my turning chauffeur? I'm not a bad one; you ask our man. Who knows, perhaps driving an automobile is my real gift!"

Of course, her companion's good humor again put her in the wrong, although Barbara knew that she was wrong in any case. For what possible right had she, after having known Dick Thornton less than a week, to undertake to tell him what he should or should not do? It was curious what a fighting instinct he had immediately aroused in her! She felt that she would almost like to hit him in order to make him wake up and realize that there was something in life besides being handsome and good-natured and smiling lazily upon the world.

However, Barbara now clasped her hands together, church fashion, inclining her curly head.

"Beg pardon again. After all, what should a Prince Charming be except a Prince Charming?" she murmured. "You are a kind of liberal education. I've lived such a work-a-day life, I can't understand why it seems so dreadful to you and your family to do the work one loves in the place where it seems to be most needed. We nurses will be under orders from people older and wiser than we are. If we come close to suffering—well, one can't live very long without doing that. But I don't want to bore you; you will be rid of me for life in a little while, and I'll leave now if your mother and father feel my plans are affecting Mildred."

"You will do no such thing." Dick's voice was curt and less polite than usual, but it was certainly decisive and so ended the discussion.

A few minutes later, apparently in a happier frame of mind, Barbara Meade was about to go upstairs when at the door she turned toward her companion.

"Please don't think I fail to understand, Mr. Thornton, your not wishing Mildred to go through the discomforts and even the dangers of nursing the wounded soldiers. I suppose every nice brother naturally wishes to protect and look after his sister. I told you I had never had a brother, but you must not think for that reason I cannot appreciate what you must feel."

Then with a quick movement characteristic of her smallness and grace, Barbara was gone.

Nevertheless Dick remained in the library alone until almost dinner time.

Barbara was right in believing that he hated the thought of his sister Mildred's being away from the care and affection of her own family. Mildred might not be so handsome as he wished her and wasn't much of a talker, still there was no doubt that she was a trump in lots of ways. Besides, after all, she was one's own and only sister. Yet Dick was honest with himself. It was not Mildred alone whom he desired to protect from hardships. Absurd, of course, when the girl was almost a stranger to him, yet Barbara Meade appeared more unfitted for the task that she insisted upon undertaking than his sister. In the first place, Barbara was younger, and certainly a hundred times prettier. Then in spite of her ridiculous temper she was so tiny and looked so like a child that one could only laugh at her. Moreover—oh, well, the worst of it was, Dick felt convinced that she was just the kind of a girl he could have a delightful time with, if he had a proper chance. She had confessed to loving to dance in spite of her sarcasm. So she should have at least a few dances with him before fate swept her out of his way forever.

Ten days later, as early as nine o'clock in the morning, Mrs. Thornton's limousine was to be seen threading its way in and out among the trucks and wagons along lower Broadway on its way to the American Line steamship pier, No. 62.

Inside the car were seated Mrs. Thornton and Mildred, Judge Thornton, Dick and Barbara Meade. Behind them a taxicab piled with luggage was following. The "Philadelphia" was sailing at eleven o'clock that morning and included among her passenger list four American Red Cross nurses on their way to a mission of relief and love.

In the Thornton automobile not alone was Barbara Meade arrayed for an ocean crossing, but Mildred Thornton also appeared to be wearing a traveling outfit. More extraordinary, the greater part of the luggage on the taxicab behind them bore the initials "M. F. T." Besides, Mildred was sitting close to her father with her cheek pressed against his shoulder and holding tight to his hand, while the Judge looked entirely and completely miserable.

Should anything happen to Mildred, he, who loved her best, would be responsible. For he had finally yielded to her persuasions, upholding her in her desire, against the repeated objections of his wife and son. Just why he had come round to Mildred's wish, for the life of him the Judge could not now decide. What was happening to this world anyhow when girls, even a gentle, sweet-tempered one like Mildred, insisted on "making something of their own lives," "doing something useful," "following their own consciences and not some one's else?" Really the Judge could not at present recall with what arguments and pleadings his daughter had finally influenced him. But he did wonder why at present he should feel so utterly dejected at the thought of Mildred's leaving, when her mother appeared positively triumphant.

Yet the fact is that within the last few days Mrs. Thornton had entirely changed her original point of view. She had discovered that instead of Mildred's engaging in an enterprise both unwomanly and unbecoming, actually she was doing the most fashionable thing of the hour. Never before had Mildred received so much notice and praise. Positively her mother glowed remembering what their friends had been saying of Mildred's nobility of character. How fine it was that she had a nature that could not be satisfied with nothing save social frivolities!

Letters of introduction to a number of the best people in England had been pouring in upon them. One from Mrs. Whitehall to her sister, the Countess of Sussex, was particularly worth while. Mrs. Thornton had never before known that she dared include the writer among her friends. Moreover, Mildred had lately been receiving unexpected attentions from the young men who had never before paid her the slightest notice. Half a dozen of them within the past few days had called to say good-by and express their admiration of her pluck. Two or three had declared themselves openly envious of her. For if there were great things going on in the world, no matter how tragic and dreadful, one would feel tremendously worth while to be right on the spot and able to judge for oneself.

Then Dick had reported that Mildred had been more than a halfway belle at a dance that he had insisted upon his sister and their visitor attending before they shut themselves off from all amusements. Such a lot of fellows wanted to talk to Mill about her plans that they seemed not to care that she could not dance any better.

Although there were only between fifty and sixty passengers booked for sailing on the "Philadelphia's" list, the big dock was crowded with freight of every kind.

On an adjoining dock there was a tremendous stamping of horses. Not far off one of the Atlantic Transport boats was being rapidly transformed into a gigantic stable. Its broad passenger decks were being divided into hundreds of box stalls. Into the hold immensely heavy boxes were being hoisted with derricks and cranes. The whole atmosphere of the New York Harbor front appeared to have changed. Where once there used to be people about to sail for Europe now there appeared to be things taking their place. No longer were pleasure-loving Americans crossing the ocean, but the product of their lands and their hands.

However, Mildred and Barbara gave only a cursory attention to these impersonal matters, and Mildred's family very little more. They were deeply interested in a meeting which was soon to take place.

Their little party was to consist of four American nurses sent out to assist the British Red Cross wherever their services were most needed.

So far Mildred and Barbara had not even seen the other two girls. However, Judge and Mrs. Thornton had been assured that one was an older woman, who had already had some years' experience in nursing and could also act as chaperon. About the fourth girl nothing of any kind had been told them.

Therefore, within five minutes after their arrival at the wharf, Miss Moore, one of the Red Cross workers in the New York headquarters from whom the girls had received instructions, joined them. With her was a girl, or a young woman (for she might be any age between twenty or thirty) for whom Mildred and Barbara both conceived an immediate prejudice. They were not willing to call the sensation dislike, because travelers upon a humanitarian crusade must dislike no one, and especially not one of their fellow laborers.

Eugenia Peabody was the stranger's name. She had come from a small town in Massachusetts. Her clothes were severely plain, a rusty brown walking suit that must have seen long service, as well as a shabby brown coat. Then she had on an absurd hat that looked like a man's, and her hair was parted in the middle and drawn back on either side. She had handsome dark eyes, so that one could not call her exactly ugly. Only she seemed terribly cold and superior and unsympathetic.

But the fourth girl, Miss Moore explained, by some accident had failed to arrive in time for the steamer. She was to have come from Charleston, South Carolina, having made her application and sent her credentials from there. It was foolish of her to have waited until the last hour before arriving in New York. Now her train had been delayed, and as her passage had been engaged, the money would simply have to be wasted. Had the Red Cross Society known beforehand, another nurse could have taken her place.

The next hour and a half was one of painful confusion. Surely so few passengers never before had so many friends to see them off. Farewells these days meant more than partings under ordinary circumstances. No matter what pretense might be made to the contrary, in every mind, deep in every heart was the possibility that a passenger steamer might strike a floating mine.

Of course, Barbara had been forced to say her hardest farewells before leaving her home in Nebraska. Nevertheless, she could not now help sharing Mildred's emotions and those of her family. Besides, the Thorntons had been so kind to her in the past two weeks. Mrs. Thornton had apologized for blaming her for Mildred's decision, but after all it was easy to understand her feeling in the matter. Judge Thornton was one of the biggest-hearted, dearest men in the world. Then there was Dick! Of course, he was a good-for-nothing fellow who would never amount to much except to be a spoiled darling all his days! Yet certainly he was attractive and had been wonderfully sweet-tempered and courteous to her.

Even this morning he had never allowed her to feel lonely for an instant. Always he saw that she was among the groups of their friends who were showering attentions upon Mildred—books and flowers and sweets, besides various extraordinary things which she was recommended to use in her work.

Dick's farewell present Barbara thought a little curious. It was an extremely costly electric lamp mounted in silver to carry about in her pocket.

"It is to help you see your way, if you should ever get lost or have to go out at night while you are doing that plagued nursing," he whispered just as the final whistles blew and the friends of the passengers were being put ashore.

As Dick ran down the gang-plank, both Mildred and Barbara were watching him with their eyes full of tears. Suddenly he had to step aside in order not to run over a girl hurrying up the plank from the shore. She was dressed in deep mourning; her hair was of the purest gold and her eyes brown. She had two boys with her, each one of them carrying an extraordinary looking old-fashioned carpet bag of a pattern of fifty years ago.

"I regret it if I have kept you waiting," she said in a soft, drawling voice to one of the stewards who happened to be nearest the gang-plank. "I've come all the way from Charleston, South Carolina, and my train was four hours late."

The tears driven away by curiosity, Mildred and Barbara now stared at each other. Was this the fourth girl who was to accompany them as a Red Cross nurse? She looked less like a nurse than any one of them. Why, she was as fragile as possible herself, and evidently had never been away from home before in her life. Now she was under the impression that the steamer had been kept waiting for her. Certainly she was apologizing to the steward for delaying them.

Yet a glance at their older companion and both girls felt a warm companionship for the newcomer. For if Miss Peabody had been discouraged on being introduced to them, it was nothing to the disfavor she now allowed herself to show at the appearance of the fourth member of their little Red Cross band.

A little later, with deep blasts from her whistle, the "Philadelphia" began to move out. Amid much waving of handkerchiefs, both on deck and on shore, the voyage had begun.

CHAPTER IV
Making Acquaintances

"In my opinion no one of you girls will remain in Europe three months, at least not as a nurse. You are going over because of an emotion or an enthusiasm—same thing! You are too young and have not had sufficient experience for the regular Red Cross nursing. Besides, you haven't the faintest idea of what may lie ahead of you," Eugenia Peabody announced.

It was a sunshiny day, although not a calm one, yet the "Philadelphia" was making straight ahead. She was a narrow boat that pitched rather than rolled. Nevertheless, a poor sailor could scarcely be expected to enjoy the plunging she was now engaging in. It was as if one were riding a horse who rose first on his forefeet and then on his hind feet, tossing his rider relentlessly back and forth.

So, although the four Red Cross girls were seated on the upper deck in their steamer chairs and at no great distance apart, no forcible protest followed the oldest one's statement.

However, from under the shelter of her close-fitting squirrel-fur cap Barbara's blue eyes looked belligerent. She was wearing a coat of the same kind. The next moment she protested:

"Of course, we have not had the experience required for salaried nurses, and of course we are a great deal younger than you" (as Barbara was not enamored of Eugenia she made this remark with intentional emphasis). "But I don't consider it fair for you to decide for that reason we are going to be useless. The Red Cross was willing that we should help in some way, even though we can't be enrolled nurses until we have had two years' hospital work. Mildred and I have both graduated, and Nona Davis has had one year's work. Besides, soldiers, often when they are quite young boys, go forth to battle and do wonderful things. Who knows what we may accomplish? Sometimes success comes just from pluck and the ability to hold on. Right this minute you can't guess, Miss Peabody, which one of us is brave and which one may be a coward; there is no telling till the test comes."

Then after her long tirade Barbara again subsided into the depth of her chair. What a spitfire she was! Really, she must learn to control her temper, for if the four of them were to work together, they must be friends. Dick

Thornton had been right. Perhaps the wounded soldiers might have a hard time with a crosspatch for a nurse. But this Miss Peabody was so painfully superior, so "Bostonese"! Even if she *had* come only from a small Massachusetts town, it had been situated close to the sacred city, and Eugenia had been educated there. Small wonder that she had little use for a girl from far-off Nebraska!

Nevertheless, Eugenia's cheeks had crimsoned at Barbara's speech and her expression ruffled, although her hair remained as smooth as if the wind had not been blowing at the rate of sixty miles an hour.

"That is one way of looking at things," she retorted. "I suppose almost anybody willing to make sacrifices can be useful at the front these days," she conceded. "But, really, I do not consider that I am so very much older than the rest of you, even if I am acting as your chaperon. I have always looked older than I am. I was only twenty-five my last birthday and one can't be an enrolled Red Cross nurse any younger than that—at least, not in America."

"Oh, I beg pardon," Barbara replied. At the same time she was thinking that twenty-five was considerably older than eighteen and nineteen, and that before seven years had passed she expected a good many interesting things to have happened to her.

But a soft drawl interrupted Barbara's train of thought. Issuing from the depth of a steamer blanket it had a kind of smothered sound.

"I am older than the rest of you think. I am twenty-one," the voice announced. "I only seem younger because I am stupid and have never been away from home before. My father was quite old when I was born, so I have nearly always taken care of him. He was a general in the Confederate army. I've heard nothing but war-talk my whole life and the great things the southern women sacrificed for the soldiers. My mother I don't know a great deal about."

For a moment Nona seemed to be hesitating. "My father died a year ago. There was nobody to care a great deal what became of me except some old friends. So when this war broke out, I felt I must help if only the least little bit. I sold everything I had for my expenses, except my father's old army pistol and the ragged half of a Confederate flag; these I brought along with me. But please forgive my talking so much about myself. It seemed to me if we were to be together that we ought to know a little about one another. I haven't told you everything. My father's family, even though we were poor——"

- 23 -

Nona paused, and Barbara smiled. Even Eugenia melted slightly, while Mildred took hold of the hand that lay outside the steamer blanket.

"Don't trouble to tell us anything you would rather not, Miss Davis," she returned. "We have only to see and talk to you to have faith in you. Of course, we don't have to tell family *secrets*; that would be expecting rather too much."

With a sigh suggesting relief Nona Davis glanced away from her companions toward the water. The girl was like a white and yellow lily, with her pale skin, pure gold hair and brown eyes with golden centers. In her life she had never had an intimate girl friend. Now with all her heart she was hoping that her new acquaintances might learn to care for her. And yet if they knew what had kept her shut away from other girls, perhaps they too might feel the old prejudice!

But suddenly happier and stronger than since their sailing, Nona straightened up. Then she arranged her small black felt hat more becomingly.

"I don't want to talk *all* the time, only really I am stronger than I look. As I know French pretty well, perhaps I may at least be useful in that way."

The girl's expression suddenly altered. A reserve that was almost haughtiness swept over it. For she had been the first to notice a fellow passenger walking up and down the deck in front of them. She had now stopped at a place where she could overhear what they were saying. The girls had agreed not to discuss their plans on shipboard. It seemed wisest not to let their fellow passengers know that they were going abroad to help with Red Cross nursing. For in consequence there might be a great deal of talk, questions would be asked, unnecessary advice given. Besides, the girls did not yet know what duties were to be assigned them. They were ordered to go to a British Red Cross, deliver their credentials and await results.

So everything that might have betrayed their mission had been carefully packed away in their trunks and bags. Moreover, in the hold of the steamer there were great wooden packing cases of gauze bandaging, medicines and antiseptics which Judge Thornton had given Mildred and Barbara as his farewell offering. These were to be presented to the hospital where the girls would be stationed.

Now, although Nona Davis had become aware of the curiosity of the traveler who had taken up a position near them, Eugenia Peabody had not. So before the younger girl could warn her she exclaimed:

"Hope you won't think I meant to be disagreeable. Of course, you may turn out better nurses than I; perhaps experience *isn't* everything."

There was no doubt this time that Eugenia intended being agreeable, yet her manner was still curt. She seemed one of the unfortunate persons without charm, who manage to antagonize just when they wish to be agreeable.

At this moment the stranger made no further effort at keeping in the background. Instead she walked directly toward the four girls.

"I chanced to overhear you saying something about Red Cross nursing," she began. "Can it be that you are going over to help care for the poor soldiers? How splendid of you! I do hope you don't mind my being interested?"

Of course the girls did mind. However, there was nothing to do under the circumstances. Barbara alone made a faint effort at denial. Eugenia simply looked annoyed because she had been the one who had betrayed them. Mildred showed surprise. But Nona Davis answered in a well-bred voice that seemed to put undesirable persons at a tremendous distance away:

"As long as you did overhear what we were saying, would you mind our not discussing the question with you. We have an idea that we prefer keeping our plans a secret among ourselves."

Yet neither Nona's words nor her manner had the desired effect. The stranger sat down on the edge of a chair that happened to be near.

"That is all right, my dear, if you prefer I shall not mention it. Only there is no reason why *I* should not know. I am a much older woman than any of you, and I too am going abroad because of this horrible war, though not to do the beautiful work you expect to do."

At this moment the newcomer smiled in a kind yet anxious fashion, so that three of the girls were propitiated. After all, she was a middle-aged woman of about fifty, quietly and inexpensively dressed, and she had a timid, confidential manner. Somehow one felt unaccountably sorry for her.

"I am traveling with my son," she explained. "You may have noticed the young man in dark glasses. My son is a newspaper correspondent and is now going to try to get into the British lines. He was ill when the war broke out or we should have crossed over sooner. There may be difficulties about our arrangements. After his illness I was not willing that he should go into danger unless I was near him. Then his eyes still trouble him so greatly that I sometimes help with his work."

She leaned over and whispered more confidentially than ever:

"I am Mrs. John Curtis, my son is Brooks Curtis, you may be familiar with his name. I only wanted to say that if at any time I can be useful, either on shipboard or if we should run across each other in Europe, please don't hesitate to call upon me. I had a daughter of my own once and had she lived I have no doubt she would now be following your example."

Actually the older woman's eyes were filling with tears, and although the girls felt embarrassed by her confidences they were touched and grateful, all except Nona Davis, who seemed in a singularly difficult humor.

"You are awfully kind, Mrs. Curtis, I am sure," Mildred was murmuring, when Nona asked unexpectedly:

"Mrs. Curtis, if your son has trouble with his eyes, I wonder why I have so often seen him with his glasses off gazing out to sea through a pair of immense telescope glasses? I should think the strain would be bad for him."

Half a moment the older woman hesitated, then leaning over toward the little group, she whispered:

"You must not be frightened by anything I tell you. Sailing under the American flag we of course ought to feel perfectly safe, but you girls must know the possibilities we face these days. I think perhaps because I am with him my son may be a little too anxious. However, I shall certainly tell him he is not to take off his glasses again during the voyage. You are right; it may do him harm."

A few moments later Mrs. Curtis strolled away. But by this time Nona Davis was sitting bolt upright with more color in her face than she had shown since the hour of her arrival.

"I do hope we may not have to see a great deal of Mrs. Curtis," she volunteered.

"Why not?" Mildred asked. "I thought her very nice. I feel that my mother would like us to be friends with an older woman; she might be able to give us good advice. Please tell us why you object to her?"

The other girl shook her head.

"I am sure I don't know. I don't suppose I have any *real* reason. You see, I don't often have reasons for things; at least, not the kind I know how to explain to other people. But my old colored mammy used to say I was a 'second sighter.'"

CHAPTER V
"Lady Dorian"

V ery carefully the young man in the dark glasses must have considered which one of the four American girls traveling together he might expect to find most worth while. Then he chose Mildred Thornton.

And this was odd, for to a casual observer Mildred was the least good looking and the least gay of the four. Even Eugenia, in spite of her severe manner, had a certain handsomeness and under softening influences might improve both in appearance and disposition.

Nevertheless, it was with Mildred that Nona Davis, coming out of her stateroom half an hour before dinner, discovered the young man talking.

It happened that Nona and Mildred shared the same stateroom while the two other girls were just across the narrow passageway. As the decks were apt to be freer from other passengers at this hour preceding dinner, they had arranged for a quiet walk. But now, although seeing her plainly enough, Nona soon realized that Mildred had no idea of keeping her engagement. She was far too deeply engrossed in her new companion. It was annoying, this eternal feminine habit of choosing any kind of masculine society in preference to the most agreeable feminine! However, Nona made no sign or protest. She merely betook herself to the opposite side of the boat and started a solitary stroll.

There was no one to interfere and she was virtually alone, as this happened to be the windy, disagreeable portion of the deck. Of their meeting with Mrs. Curtis the day before no one had spoken since, but now Nona could not help recalling her own impression. She was sorry for her sudden prejudice and more so for her open expression of it.

"I must try and not distrust people," she thought remorsefully. "Suspicion made my father's life bitter and shut me away from other girls. So, should circumstances compel us to meet this Mrs. Curtis and her son (and one never knows when chance may throw strangers together), why I shall never, never say a word against them."

Nona was looking out toward a curious purple and smoke-colored sunset at the edge of the western sky as she made this resolution. Perhaps because the vision before her had somehow suggested the smoke of battle and the strange, dreadful world toward which they were voyaging. Eugenia was right. No one of them could dream of what lay ahead.

For a moment she had paused and was standing with one hand resting on the ship's railing when to her surprise Mildred Thornton's voice sounded close beside her.

"Nona, I want to introduce Mr. Curtis," she began. "We have been trying to find you. Oh, I confess I did see you a few moments ago, only I pretended I had not. Mr. Curtis was telling me something so interesting I did not wish to interrupt him for fear he might not repeat it."

Mildred's eyes had darkened with excitement and she was speaking in a hushed voice, although no one appeared to be near.

Nona Davis extended her hand to the young man. "My name is Davis," she began. "Miss Thornton forgot to mention it, for although we have known each other but a few days we are already using our first names."

Then she struggled with a sense of distaste. The hand that received hers was large and bony and curiously limp and unresponsive. Afterwards Nona studied the young fellow's face. It was difficult to get a vital impression of him when his eyes were so hidden from view, but of one thing she became assured—he was not particularly young.

He was tall and had a fringe of light brown hair around a circular space where the hair was plainly growing thinner. His face was smooth, his mouth irregular and he had a large inquiring nose. Indeed, Nona decided that the young man suggested a human question mark, although his eyes— and eyes can ask more questions than the tongue—were partly concealed.

"Mr. Curtis has been a war correspondent before," Mildred went on, showing an enthusiasm that was unusual with her. "He has just returned from the war in Mexico and has been telling me of the horrors down there."

"But I thought," Nona Davis replied and then hesitated. What she was thinking was, that Mrs. Curtis had mentioned her son's long illness. This may have followed his return; he was not particularly healthy looking. Not knowing exactly how to conclude her sentence, she was glad to have Mildred whisper:

"Mr. Curtis says he has secret information that our ship is carrying supplies for the Allies. Oh, of course we are on an American passenger boat and it sounds incredible, but then nothing is past belief these days."

Nevertheless, the other girl shook her head doubtingly. She was a little annoyed at the expression of entire faith with which Mildred gazed upon their latest acquaintance. She wondered if Mildred were the type of girl who believed anything because a *man* told her it was true. Odd that she did not feel that way herself, when all her life she had been taught to depend wholly upon masculine judgment. But there were odd stirrings of revolt in the little southern girl of which she was not yet aware. She appeared flowerlike and gentle in her old-fashioned black costume. One would have thought she had no independence of body or mind, but like a flower could be swayed by any wind.

"Oh, I don't expect we are carrying anything except hospital supplies of the same kind your father is sending, Mildred," she answered. Then turning apologetically toward the young newspaper man: "I beg your pardon, I didn't mean to doubt your word, only your information."

However, Brooks Curtis was not paying any attention to her. Instead he was gazing reproachfully at Mildred and at the same time attempting to smile.

"Is that the way you keep a secret, Miss Thornton?" he demanded. "Of course, your friend is right. I have no absolute information. Who has in these war times? I only wanted you to realize that in case trouble arises you are to count on my mother and me."

He appeared to make the last remark idly and without emphasis, notwithstanding Mildred flushed uneasily.

"You don't mean that there may be an explosion on shipboard or a danger of that kind," she expostulated. "It sounds absurd, I know, but I am nervous about the water. I have crossed several times before, but always with my father and brother."

While she was speaking Nona Davis had slipped her arm reassuringly inside her new friend's. "Nonsense," she said quietly. "Mr. Curtis is trying to tease us." Then deliberately she drew Mildred away and commenced their postponed walk. It was just as well, because at this instant Mrs. Curtis had come on deck to join her son.

A little farther along and Nona pressed her delicate cheek against her taller companion's sleeve. "For heaven's sake don't let Miss Peabody know you are afraid of an accident at sea when you are going into the midst of a world tragedy," she whispered. "Eugenia believes we are hopeless enough as it is. But whenever you are frightened, Mildred—and of course we must all be now and then—won't you confide in me?" Nona's tones and the expression of her golden brown eyes were wistful and appealing.

"You see, it is queer, but I don't fear what other people do. I have certain foolish terrors of my own that I may tell you of some day. For one thing, I am afraid of ghosts. I don't exactly believe in them, but I was brought up by an old colored mammy who instilled many of her superstitions into me."

Their conversation ended at this because Barbara and Eugenia Peabody were now walking toward them, both looking distinctly unamiable. It was unfortunate that the two girls should be rooming together. They were most uncongenial, and so far spent few hours in each other's society without an altercation of some kind.

Nona smiled at their approach. "And east is east and west is west, and never the twain shall meet," she quoted mischievously. Then she became sober again because she too had a wholesome awe of the eldest member of their party, and Eugenia's eyes held fire.

Some powerful current of electricity must have been at work in that portion of the universe through which the "Philadelphia" was ploughing her way that evening.

For as soon as they entered the ship's dining room the four girls became aware of a tense atmosphere which had never been there before. They chanced to be a few moments late, so that the other voyagers were already seated.

Mildred Thornton, by special courtesy, was on the Captain's right hand and Barbara Meade on his left (this attention was a tribute to Judge Thornton's position in New York); Nona was next Mildred and Eugenia next Barbara.

Then on Nona Davis' other side sat a beautiful woman of perhaps thirty in whom the four girls were deeply interested. But not because she had been in the least friendly with them, or with any one else aboard ship, not even with Captain Miller, who was a splendid big Irishman, one of the most popular officers in the service, and to whom the Red Cross girls were already deeply attached.

Four days had passed since the "Philadelphia" sailed and the voyage was now more than half over. But except that she appeared on the passenger list as "Lady Dorian," no one knew anything of the young woman's identity. Her name was English, and yet she did not look English and spoke, when conversation was forced upon her, with a slightly foreign accent, which might be Russian, or possibly German. However, she never talked to anyone and only came to the table at dinner time, rarely appearing upon deck and never without her maid.

But tonight as the girls took their places at the dinner table it was evident that Lady Dorian had been speaking and that her conversation had been upon a subject which Captain Miller had requested no one mention during the course of the voyage—the war!

Every one of the sixteen persons at the Captain's table looked flushed and excited, Mrs. Curtis at the farther end was in tears, and an English banker, Sir George Paxton, who had lately been in Washington on public business, appeared in danger of apoplexy.

"What is the trouble, Captain?" Barbara whispered, as soon as she had half a chance. She was a special favorite of Captain Miller's and they had claimed cousinship at once on account of their Irish ancestry.

"Bombs!" the Captain murmured, "not real ones; worse kind, conversational bombs. That Curtis fellow started the question of whether the United States had the right to furnish ammunition to the Allies. Then Lady Dorian began some kind of peace talk, to which the Englishman objected. Can't tell you exactly what it was all about, as I had to try to quiet things down. They may start to blowing up my ship next; this war talk makes sane people turn suddenly crazy."

A movement made Barbara glance across the table. Although dinner was only beginning, Lady Dorian had risen and was leaving.

No wonder the girls admired her appearance. Barbara swallowed a little sigh of envy. Never, no never, could she hope to go trailing down a long room with all eyes turned upon her, looking so beautiful and cold and distinguished. This was one of the many trials of being small and darting about so quickly and having short hair and big blue eyes like a baby's. One's hair could grow, but, alas, not one's self, after a certain age!

Lady Dorian was probably about five feet seven, which is presumably the ideal height for a woman, since it is the height of the Venus de Milo. She had gray eyes with black brows and lashes and dark hair that was turning gray. This was perfectly arranged, parted at the side and in a low coil. Tonight she had on a gown of black satin and chiffon. Though she wore no jewels there was no other woman present with such an air of wealth and distinction.

The instant she had disappeared, however, Mrs. Curtis turned to her son, speaking in a voice sufficiently loud to be heard by every one at the Captain's table.

"I don't believe for a moment that woman's name is 'Lady Dorian.' She is most certainly not an English woman. Even if she is married to an Englishman she is undoubtedly pro-German in her sentiments. I shouldn't be surprised if she is—well, most anything."

Brooks Curtis flushed, vainly attempting to silence his mother. Evidently she was one of the irrepressible people who would not be silenced. The Red Cross girls need not have been flattered or annoyed by her attentions.

She appeared one of the light-minded women who go about talking to everybody, apparently confiding their own secrets and desiring other confidences in exchange. She seemed to be harmless though trying.

But the Captain's great voice boomed down the length of the table.

"No personalities, please. Who is going to tell me the best story before I go back on duty? Perhaps Miss Davis will tell us some negro stories!"

Nona blushed uncomfortably. She was shy at being suddenly made the center of observation, yet she appreciated the Captain's intention.

Nevertheless, and in spite of her best efforts, the disagreeable atmosphere in the dining room remained. Mrs. Curtis was not alone in her suspicion of the vanished woman. There was not another person at the table who did not in a greater or less degree share it. Lady Dorian was strangely reserved about her history in these troublous war times. Then she had been trying to keep her point of view concealed. However, to the Red Cross girls, or at least to the three younger ones, she was a romantic, fascinating figure. One could easily conceive of her in a tragic role. Secretly both Barbara and Nona decided to try to know her better if this were possible without intrusion.

An hour after dinner and the Red Cross girls were in bed. There was nothing to do to amuse oneself, as the lights must be extinguished by half-past eight o'clock. The Captain meant to take no risks of over-zealous German cruisers or submarines.

CHAPTER VI
A Trial of Fire

A t dawn Barbara awakened perfectly refreshed. She felt that she had been asleep for an indefinite length of time, and although she made a slight effort, further sleep was impossible. How long before the hour for her bath, and how stuffy their little stateroom had become!

Barbara occupied the upper berth. Swinging herself a little over the side she saw that Eugenia was breathing deeply. Asleep Barbara conceded that Eugenia might almost be called handsome. Her features were well cut, her dark hair smooth and abundant, and her expression peaceful. However, even with consciousness somewhere on the other side of things Eugenia still looked like an old maid. Barbara wondered if she had ever had an admirer in her life. Although wishing to give Eugenia the benefit of the doubt, she scarcely thought so. It would have made her less difficult surely!

Twice Barbara turned over and burrowed her curly brown head in her pillow. She dared not even move very strenuously for fear of waking her companion and arousing her ire. Of course, it was irritating to be awakened at daylight, but then how was she to endure the stupidity and stuffiness of their room without some entertainment? If only she could read or study her French, but there was not yet sufficient daylight, and turning on the electric light was too perilous.

Staring up at the ceiling only a few feet above her head where the life belts protruded above the white planking, Barbara had a sudden vision of what the dawn must be like at this hour upon the sea. How she longed for the rose and silver spectacle. Had she not been wishing to see the sunrise every morning since coming aboard ship? And here at last was her opportunity. Should Eugenia be disagreeable enough to awaken she must simply face the music.

Noiselessly Barbara's bare toes were extended over the side of the berth and then she reached the floor with almost no perceptible sound. She was so tiny and light she could do things more quietly than other people. A few moments later she had on her shoes and stockings, her underclothing and her heavy coat, with the little squirrel cap over her hair. It would be cold up on deck. But one need not be particularly careful of one's costume, since there would probably be no one about except a weary officer changing his watch. It was too early for the sailors to have begun washing the decks, else she must have heard the noise before this. Their stateroom was below the promenade deck.

As Barbara closed the outside door of their room she heard Eugenia stirring. But she slipped away without her conscience being in the least troublesome. If Eugenia was at last aroused, she would not be there to be reproached. The thought rather added zest to her enterprise. Besides, it was wrong for a trained nurse to be a sleepy-head; one ought to be awake and ready at all times for emergencies. Had Barbara needed spurs to her own ideals of helpfulness in her nursing, she had found them in Eugenia's and in Dick Thornton's openly expressed doubts of her. Whatever came, she must make good or perish.

The deck was not inspiring. Barbara had anticipated the sunrise. Over toward the eastern line of the horizon the darkness had lifted, but as yet there was no color. The sky and water were curiously the same, a translucent gray. One felt but could not see the light beneath. The ship was making steady progress because there was now no wind and the surface of the sea appeared perfectly smooth.

For a few moments the girl walked up and down to keep warm and to wait for the dawn. Then she found her steamer chair, pulled it into such a position that it commanded an unbroken view of the horizon, and covering herself with steamer blankets, stared straight ahead.

A little later at some distance away she saw something black thrust itself above the surface of the water and then disappear. It looked like a gigantic nose.

Barbara's breath began to come more quickly and grasping hold of the arms of her chair she half arose. But now the black object had appeared again and was coming closer to the ship. Of course, she had been thinking of a submarine. However, she could now see that the creature was being followed by a perfectly irrepressible family connection of porpoises, dipping their heads under the waves, flirting their tails in a picturesque fashion and dancing a kind of sea tango.

Then the porpoises disappeared. Calmer than she had ever imagined grew the entire face of the water, stiller the atmosphere. This was the strange moment of silence that follows the breaking of each new day. Perchance it may be nature's time for silent prayer.

Anyhow Barbara was familiar enough with this moment on land. It is the moment in nursing the sick when one must be most watchful and strong. Then life struggles to get away from the exhausted body on strange new quests of its own. But Barbara had never faced a dawn upon the sea.

She wished now that she had called Mildred and Nona; perhaps they too would have cared for the oncoming spectacle. Then Barbara forgot herself and her soul filled with wonder. The sun had risen. It threw great streams of light across the sky like giant banners, of such colors as no army of the world has ever fought under, and these showed a second time upon the mirror of the sea. A few moments they stayed like this, and then melted together into red and violet and rose, until after a while the day's serener blue conquered and held the sky.

Weary from the beauty and her own emotion, Barbara closed her eyes, meaning to go downstairs as soon as the sailors came on deck. However, she must have fallen asleep for a few moments. Reopening her eyes she had a distinct conviction that she must be dreaming. Undoubtedly she was seeing an impossible thing. A few feet away from her chair, forcing its way between the planks of the floor, was a small spiral column of smoke.

It could not be smoke, of course, one felt convinced of that; yet it was odd that it should look and behave so much like smoke.

Barbara got herself disentangled from her steamer rugs and jumped to her feet. This was a reliable method of waking oneself up. She took a single step forward and then turned and ran along the deck to the stairway more swiftly than she had ever run in her life. She was not mistaken, it *was* smoke issuing from underneath the deck. Possibly this meant nothing serious, no one in the world could know less of a ship than she did. Then there was a possibility that their steamer might be on fire, when the crew must be alarmed at once. Barbara had not studied to become a trained nurse without learning coolness. Under no circumstances must she cry fire and so create a panic. She had no other conscious thought except that she must find one of the ship's officers or sailors and give the alarm.

But before she was more than half along the companion way the girl heard a noise like the explosion of a muffled gun. Straightway she pitched face forward down the steps. Nevertheless she was not hurt. The next instant she was up and running along the hall, reached the door of her own stateroom just as Eugenia flung the door open. At the same time Nona's and Mildred's white faces stared forth.

"Put on some clothes quickly. There has been an accident, I don't know how serious," Barbara commanded. But the information was scarcely necessary. Already the ship seemed alive with running feet. Commands were being shouted, while as by magic stewards were urging the passengers to be calm, insisting there was no danger. The trouble was probably not serious, yet they must be prepared.

Barbara entered her stateroom. Her pocketbook and a few valuables she must try to save in case they had to take to the life-boats.

In the middle of the room she found Eugenia Peabody in her nightgown, shaking with terror and making not the least effort to get dressed.

Barbara forgot the respect due to their chaperon. Deliberately she seized her by the shoulders and began shaking her severely. It was absurd, or would have been under other circumstances. Eugenia was so much taller and larger and older than her companion that it looked as if a governess were being disciplined by a small pupil.

However, the younger girl was terribly in earnest. "Don't lose your senses," she protested angrily. Then darting about the tiny room in an incredible time she secured the other girl's clothes and got her into them in a haphazard fashion.

Finally Eugenia fled to the closed door, only to be dragged back by her companion.

"Your shoes and stockings, please, Miss Peabody," Barbara argued determinedly. "There is no immediate danger or we would be warned. Now let us find the other girls. Remember we are Red Cross nurses and not young society women." If the ship had been sinking Barbara Meade felt that she must have fired this sarcasm. But really Eugenia was so frightened she was beginning to like her better. It was human to be frightened; she was terrified herself. But it would do no good to go to pieces.

Nona and Mildred were both ready. So the four girls went together into the big saloon where all the other ship's passengers were gathering.

The fire was not supposed to be dangerous. The men were fighting it, but they must wait to find out if it could be controlled. No, no one had an idea of what had caused the explosion.

Of course, a number of the women were crying and some of the men were white as ghosts, others were laughing foolishly.

Mrs. Curtis was distinguishing herself by having an attack of hysteria in the arms of her son. Very quietly Mildred Thornton went up and took hold of the older woman's hand.

"Let us find a seat somewhere and talk," she said soothingly. But Mrs. Curtis did not wait to be seated.

"You see," she sobbed, clutching Mildred's arm, "the explosion occurred right in our corridor. I was asleep when suddenly there was a dreadful noise and my room filled with smoke. Brooks managed to get to me the next instant. No one could have felt the shock as much as I did, except Lady Dorian. Her room is across from mine and I believe she was slightly injured. Has anyone seen her?"

At this moment the second officer entered the saloon. His face was white, but his lips wore a steady, automatic smile.

"Captain Miller wishes me to inform you that there is no further danger," he shouted. "The 'Philadelphia' will continue her journey to Liverpool. We have discovered the cause of the fire and the men have smothered it. The passengers will kindly return to their staterooms and breakfast will be served at as early an hour as possible."

At this moment Barbara Meade felt a light touch on her arm. Mildred was over in a corner with Brooks Curtis and his mother; Eugenia was talking to a number of equally excited strangers. So it was Nona Davis who said:

"Don't you think, Barbara, we might go and offer our services to Lady Dorian? If she really is hurt, as Mrs. Curtis said, perhaps we may be able to do something for her. In any case I feel we ought to show our interest. She is not popular on board ship, and even if she resents our coming I think we shall have done the kindest thing."

Barbara nodded her agreement, glancing admiringly at Nona Davis. Nona was such an embodiment of refinement in manner and appearance that it would be difficult to treat her ungraciously.

CHAPTER VII
The Landing

"I t is too horrible and too absurd!" said Barbara, a little brokenly.

The "Philadelphia" was now not far from Liverpool, proceeding with infinite caution through the submarine and mine-haunted waters. In great letters her name was painted on either side and never did the Stars and Stripes float more conspicuously overhead.

Dressed for the arrival in England, Barbara and Nona were standing side by side at a little distance from their fellow passengers. Mildred was seated with the newspaper correspondent and his mother, and Eugenia was talking with a good deal of interest to the English banker.

Nona did not answer the other girl's speech immediately. She had frowned, started to say something and then evidently changed her mind. Both she and Barbara looked absurdly young and girlish for the work ahead of them. Moreover, in their different ways they were typically American, although their types were not the familiar ones known to most Europeans.

Barbara had the vivacity, the alertness and the "goaheadiveness" of the western girl. And in spite of being only a miniature physical edition of these traits of character she was not miniature in any other sense. Nona was more difficult to explain. She appeared so exactly what she had been brought up to be and yet she might surprise one by unexpected characteristics. She was almost too refined in her manner and aspect; it gave her a look of delicacy and diffidence. And in some ways Nona was shy. Nevertheless, there was a possibility that she might have the strength and mettle which one is supposed to find in a thoroughbred horse.

Finally she returned in her quiet drawl, which did not make her remark less emphatic:

"Don't worry, Barbara dear, at least not more than you can help. It has been dreadful to have Lady Dorian a prisoner for these last few days, yet Captain Miller has been as polite as he could be under the circumstances. You see, as soon as the men discovered that the explosion on the ship had been intentional, there had to be a scapegoat. And you know Lady Dorian *is* mysterious. She won't say what her real name is and she won't surrender the odd iron box of papers that she is carrying with her. Besides, the accident did start either inside or near her stateroom. The small safe which must have contained the explosive was found not far away."

Nona paused. Though Barbara had listened politely enough she now shrugged her shoulders, saying reproachfully, "Why, Nona, how odd you are! Actually you talk as if you believed Lady Dorian guilty! Always before you have been her staunchest champion. Besides, she seems to have taken a great fancy to you. Now if Mildred had been speaking I should have understood. She has been so influenced by Mrs. Curtis, or by her son; but——"

A peculiar expression crossed her companion's face which at the instant silenced Barbara.

"Oh, no, I don't think Lady Dorian guilty; the idea is ridiculous," Nona whispered. "So far as we have been able to judge, she is one of the gentlest people in the world. The box of papers may prove that she is sacrificing herself for her country in some strange way. She won't be able to keep them hidden once she lands. Captain Miller says that they will have to be given up to the proper authorities. He did not insist upon her relinquishing them upon his ship, because he had as much as he could do to get us ashore in safety. Besides, Lady Dorian is a woman. Captain Miller says an Irishman had best leave such a situation alone. I am not sure he really suspects her."

At this moment, hearing footsteps near, Nona Davis turned from looking out toward the sea.

Approaching the place where they stood was the woman about whom they had just been talking. She was dressed in dark-blue cloth with a small hat of the same shade trimmed in a single darker feather. Behind her came her maid carrying a long coat, and on either side of her were two of the ship's officers. They were entirely respectful, although never getting any distance away. However, they need not have been fearful, because the woman's hands were locked together with a small steel chain.

She seemed pale and ill and yet, oddly enough, neither frightened nor ashamed.

But the sight of her handcuffs had set Barbara's cheeks flaming indignantly. Yet they aroused an odd point of view. Could Nona be right in her suggestion that people commit strange crimes in the name of country in times of war, crimes from which their souls would have shrunk in horror during peace? No, guilt of any kind was impossible to imagine in connection with their new friend. In a sense Lady Dorian had become their friend, since she and Nona had been helping to care for her. Lady Dorian had been ill ever since the night of the explosion and the accusation following upon it.

However, while she had been thinking, Nona, who was usually slower in her movements, had crossed over and slipped her arm inside the older woman's.

They made a queer, effective picture standing together. Barbara was conscious of it before joining them.

They were both women of refinement, who looked as if they should be sheltered from every adversity. Nona was dressed in shabby black, since all the money she had was being devoted to her expenses. Lady Dorian's costume suggested wealth. Nona was delicately pretty, with promise of beauty to come, while the older woman was at the zenith of her loveliness. Nevertheless, something they had in common. Barbara's western common sense asserted itself. "Perhaps it is because they both belong to 'first families,'" she thought wickedly, and wondered if this were a good or evil fortune. Certainly until she reached them, Nona and Lady Dorian were as completely alone as if the ship's deck had been a desert island.

Five minutes before several dozen persons had been loitering in the neighborhood, impatiently watching and praying to be landed as soon as possible. But as Lady Dorian advanced they had retreated. Perhaps they had meant it kindly, for it is a painful shock to see a fellow being a prisoner. Lady Dorian had been mistrusted, but she had not yet been condemned. Suspicion is not evidence.

However, the little group did not remain alone for long, for soon after both girls beheld Eugenia Peabody walking resolutely toward them. She happened to have been born a determined character, and her nursing had developed rather than diminished her determination.

Instantly Barbara and Nona became aware of Eugenia's intention and longed to frustrate it. But they both felt powerless, because Eugenia did not speak or even look at them. Her dark eyes were leveled straight at Lady Dorian. She appeared righteous and severe, but at the same time impressive.

Moreover, as soon as she began talking the older woman flushed and for the first time the tears came into her eyes.

"I don't wish to be rude or unkind, Lady Dorian," Eugenia remarked stiffly, "but I do ask you to cease any suggestion of intimacy with Miss Meade or Miss Davis. They have told you, of course, that we are now on our way to nurse the wounded British soldiers. Well, I am not for an instant accusing you of being a spy or having anything to do with the accident aboard our steamer; nevertheless, you are strongly suspected. Certainly you can see for yourself how young and inexperienced Barbara Meade and Nona Davis both are. They are in my charge and must not start their work of nursing under any cloud. By and by if you are cleared and we should happen to meet again, why then of course if you liked you could be friendly. Now——"

Eugenia stopped, but there was no doubting what she meant. Although Barbara and Nona were both furiously angry at her interference and sorry for their new friend, nevertheless there was that tiresome conviction they had so often felt since sailing—Eugenia, though trying, was frequently right.

Evidently Lady Dorian thought so too. Instinctively she lifted her hands as though intending to offer one of them to Miss Peabody. But finding this impossible she dropped her dark lashes to hide her emotion and then answered as serenely as possible:

"You are entirely right, Miss Peabody, and I am to blame for not having thought before of what you have just said to me. Please believe that I *did not think*. Miss Davis and Miss Meade have been very good to me and their sympathy and care have helped me endure these last three days. I don't know many American girls, but not for a great deal would I allow my acquaintance to make things difficult for them. It would be a poor return. I shall be arrested as soon as we arrive in Liverpool, so I think we had best say farewell at once."

Lady Dorian attempted no denial and no explanation. As she finished her speech she glanced first at Nona and then at Barbara and let her eyes say her farewells; then she stepped back a few feet nearer her guards.

Deliberately Nona followed her. Apparently unconscious of the presence of any one else she lifted up her face and touched her lips to the older woman's.

"I believe in you implicitly," she murmured. "Yes, I know there are many things you do not wish to explain at present, and of course I really know nothing in the world about you. Only I feel sure that we shall some day meet again."

Nona's faith proved unfortunate. For the first time Lady Dorian showed signs of breaking down. But the next moment, smiling, she indicated a curious scroll pin that was caught in the lace of her dress.

"Will you take that, please," she whispered, "and keep it until you have better reason for your faith in me?"

Following Eugenia, Barbara glanced curiously at Nona Davis. She was not easy to comprehend. After all, she it was who had emphasized all the reasons for doubting their new friend and then declared her belief in her entire innocence. It was merely that her faith did not depend on outward circumstances. Barbara wondered if she herself were equally as convinced. Then her conflicting sensations annoyed her. As usual, she began quarreling with Eugenia Peabody.

"If you are taking us to join Mildred and the Curtis family, Eugenia, then frankly I prefer other society. Nona and I had decided that we wished to be by ourselves when we first see the coasts of England. But so long as you feel you must be so terribly careful about chaperoning us I would like to say that we know nothing about Brooks Curtis or Mrs. Curtis except what they have told us, and Mildred Thornton has been almost exclusively in their society for the past few days." Barbara tried to smile, but she looked very tiny and forlorn. She was homesick and the parting with Lady Dorian had been disturbing. Besides, Mildred was Dick Thornton's sister and she had more or less promised Dick to try and look after her. Could anything much more disastrous occur than to have Mildred become interested in an unknown and presumably poor newspaper reporter? Certainly Brooks Curtis showed no signs of being either rich or famous in spite of his mother's claims for him. Then the thought of Mrs. Thornton's anger made Barbara wish to sigh and smile at the same time.

CHAPTER VIII
A Meeting

The four Red Cross girls were walking about in one of the most beautiful gardens in England. It was late afternoon and they were already dressed for dinner.

The Countess of Sussex, to whom they had been introduced by her sister in New York City, had invited them down from London for a few days before leaving for their work among the soldiers. In another thirty-six hours they were expecting to cross the Channel.

Of the four girls, Nona Davis seemed most to have altered in her appearance since leaving the ship. Indeed, no one could have dreamed that she could suddenly have become so pretty. But she had been half-way ill all the time of their crossing and disturbed about a number of things. Here in England for some strange reason she felt unexpectedly at home. The formality of the life on the great country estate, the coldness and dignity of many of the persons to whom they had been presented, the obsequiousness of the servants, troubled her not at all. And this in spite of the fact that the other three girls, although disguising the emotion as well as they knew how, were in a state of being painfully critical of England and the English. Possibly for this very reason Nona had made the best impression, although the letters of introduction which they had so far used had been originally given to Mildred Thornton.

But in a way perhaps Nona was more like an English girl than the others. She had lived the simplest kind of life in the beautiful old southern city of Charleston, she and her father and one old colored woman, almost lost in the big, shabby house that sheltered them. And they had been tragically poor. Nevertheless, a generation before Nona's ancestors had been accustomed to an existence of much the same kind as the English people about them, although a much more friendly one, with negro servants taking the place of white and with a stronger bond of affection than of caste.

This afternoon Nona felt almost as if she were in her own rose garden in Charleston, grown a hundred times larger and more beautiful. She walked a little ahead of the other three girls, almost unconscious of their presence and dreaming of her own shut-in childhood and the home she had sold in order to give her services to the wounded in this war.

Yet she looked as remote from the thought of war and its horrors as one could possibly imagine. She had on a white muslin dress made with a short waist and long full skirt; a piece of old lace belonging to her father's mother, an old-time Virginia belle, crossed over her slight bosom, was fastened with a topaz and pearl pin. Her pale gold hair was parted on one side and then coiled loosely on the crown of her head. It did not curl in the wilful fashion that Barbara's did, but seemed to wave gently. Her pallor was less noticeable than usual and the irises of her brown eyes were like the heart of the topaz. Then with an instinct for color which every normal girl has, Nona had fastened a golden rose, the *soleil d'or*, or sun of gold, at her waist. Because it was cool she also wore a scarf floating from her shoulders.

"Nona looks like this garden," Barbara remarked to her two companions, when they had stopped for a moment to examine a curiously trimmed box hedge, cut to resemble a peacock, "while I—I feel exactly like a cactus plant rooted out of a nice bare desert and transplanted in the midst of all this finery. I can feel the prickly thorns sticking out all over me. And if you don't mind and no one is listening I'd like to let the American eagle screech for a few moments. I never felt so American in my life as I have every minute since we landed. And as we have come to nurse the British I must get it out of my system somehow."

The two girls laughed, even Eugenia. Barbara had given such an amusing description of herself and her own sensations. And she did not look as if she belonged in her present environment, nevertheless, she was wearing her best dress, made by quite a superior Lincoln, Nebraska, dressmaker. It was of blue silk and white lace and yet somehow was not correct, so that Barbara really did appear like the doll Dick Thornton had once accused her of resembling.

Mildred Thornton had a suitable and beautiful costume of pearl-gray chiffon and Eugenia only a plain brown silk, neither new nor becoming. But, as she had explained to their hostess, she had not come to Europe with any thought of society, but merely in order to assist with the Red Cross nursing. Eugenia seemed to be very poor; indeed, though only one of the three other girls had any fortune, Eugenia's poverty was more apparent than Nona's. All her traveling outfit was of the poorest and she was painfully economical. But, as the Countess had declared that they were leading the simplest kind of life in the country, and because of the war doing almost no entertaining, Eugenia had consented to leave their lodgings in London for this short visit. She was particularly interested, since the smaller houses on the estate had been given over to the Belgian refugees, and Eugenia felt that this might be their opportunity for learning something of the war before actually beholding it.

The four girls were on their way now to visit several of the cottages where the Belgian women and children were located. But when the three girls had finished their few moments of conversation Nona Davis had disappeared.

"She will probably follow us a little later," Eugenia suggested; "we simply must not wait any longer, or dinner may be announced before we can get back to the castle."

However, Nona did not follow them, although she soon became conscious that the other girls had left her; indeed, saw them disappearing in the distance.

The truth is that at the present time she had no desire to see or talk with the Belgian refugees, nor did she wish any other company than her own for the next half hour.

She had been so accustomed to being alone for a great part of her time that the constant society of her new friends had tired her the least bit. Oh, she liked them immensely. It was not that, only that some natures require occasional solitude. And no one can be really lonely in a garden.

Had there been wounded Belgian soldiers on the Countess' estate Nona felt that she would have made the effort to meet them, but up to the present she had not seen an injured soldier, although soldiers of the other kind she had seen in great numbers, marching through the gray streets of London, splendid, khaki-clad fellows, handsome and serious. Even for them there had been no beating of drums, no waving of flags. Nona was thinking of this now while half of her attention was being bestowed on the beauties surrounding her. England was not making a game or a gala occasion of her part in this great war; for her it was a somber tragedy with no possible result save victory or death.

During her divided thinking Nona had wandered into a portion of the garden known as "The Maze." It was formed of a great number of rose trellises, the one overlapping the other until it was almost impossible to tell where the one ended and the other began. Nona must have walked inside for half an hour without the least desire to escape from her perfumed bower. The scene about her seemed so incredibly different from anything that she had the right to expect, she wished the impression to sink deeply into her consciousness that she might remember it in the more sorrowful days to come.

Then unexpectedly the garden came to an end and the girl stepped out onto a green lawn, with a small stone house near by which she recognized as the gardener's cottage.

Between the garden and the house, however, prone on the ground and asleep, lay a long figure.

Nona caught her breath, first from surprise and next from pity.

A heavy rug had been placed under the sleeper and a lighter one thrown over him. Evidently he had been reading and afterwards had fallen asleep, for magazines and papers were tumbled about and the cover partly tossed off.

At least, Nona could see that the figure was that of a young man of about twenty-two or three and that he must recently have been seriously ill. It was odd that under his tan his skin could yet manage to show so pallid and be so tightly drawn over his rather prominent cheek bones and nose. By his side were a pair of tall crutches and one of his long legs was heavily bandaged.

Nona was standing within a few feet of him, perfectly still, not daring to move or speak for fear of waking him. Evidently the young man was the gardener's son who had come home on a leave of absence while recovering from a wound.

But the next instant and without stirring, his eyes had opened and were gazing lazily into Nona's.

"It is the fairy story of the 'Sleeping Beauty' backwards," he began, without the least betrayal of amusement or surprise. "You see, our positions really ought to be reversed. You should be sleeping here. Then I should not in the least mind behaving as the Prince did when he woke the lovely Princess. He kissed her, I believe."

Nona was startled and a little frightened. But one could not be frightened of a boy who must have been terribly injured and was now trying to fight his way back to life with what gayety he could.

"Are you the gardener's son?" she asked, a little after Eugenia's manner and really quite foreign to her own. She had never seen a young man with such blue eyes as this one had, nor such queer brown hair that seemed to have been burned to red in spots.

"I am a son of Adam," he answered, still grave as ever, "and he was, I have been told, the earth's *first* gardener. Now tell me: Are you a Princess?"

The girl smiled a little more graciously. She had possessed very few boy friends and certainly no one of them had ever talked to her in this fashion. However, it was amusing and if it entertained the young fellow there could be no harm in their talking. Nona Davis had the poise and understanding that came of gentle birth.

So she shook her golden head gravely.

"I am not a Princess, I am sorry to spoil your fairy story. No, I am just an American girl who has come over to try and be a little useful with the Red Cross work. My friends and I met the Countess of Sussex the other day and she was kind enough to ask us down to see her place before we leave for the front."

During her speech the young man had been attempting to get himself off the ground by rising on his elbow. But even with this movement he must have wrenched his wounded leg, for immediately after he dropped back again, and although suppressing a groan, Nona could see that perspiration had broken out on his thin temples and on his smooth boyish lips.

The next instant she was down on her knees at his side. He had gotten into an abominably awkward position so that his head hung over the pillows instead of resting upon them.

How often Nona had assisted her old father in a like difficulty!

She may not have had the training of the other three American Red Cross girls, but she had practical experience and the nursing instinct.

With skill and with gentleness and without a word she now slipped her bare white arm under the stranger's shoulders and gradually drew him back into a comfortable position. Then she took her arm away again, but continued to kneel on the corner of his rug waiting to see if there were to be any signs of faintness.

There were none. Without appearing surprised or even thanking her, the young Englishman continued his fantastic conversation.

"We have turned American girls into Princesses in Europe quite an extraordinary number of times. I have wondered sometimes how they liked it, since I have been told they are all queens in their own land."

Then observing that his companion considered his remarks degenerating into foolishness, he groped about until his hand touched the book he desired.

"Forgive my nonsense," he urged penitently. "You can put it down to the fact that I have actually been reading Andersen's Fairy Tales half the afternoon. I have grown so terribly bored with everything for the past six weeks while I have been trying to get this confounded leg well enough to go back and join my regiment."

He offered the little book to Nona, and almost instinctively, as the wind scattered the pages, she glanced down upon the front leaf to discover her companion's name. There it was written in an unformed handwriting. "Robert Hume, from Mother Susan."

"Robert Hume," Nona repeated the name to herself mentally without lifting her eyes. It was a fine name, and yet it had a kind of middle class English sound like George Eliot, or Charles Dickens. Nona realized that what is known in English society as the middle class had produced most of England's greatness. Nevertheless it was surprising to find the son of a gardener possessed of so much intelligence.

He even pretended not to have noticed that she had endeavored to discover his name.

She put the book on the ground and got up on her feet again.

"I must go now," she said gently, "but it is growing late. May I not call some one to take you indoors?"

"Please," he answered, "if you will go there to the small stone house and tell Mother Susan I am awake, she will have some one look after me. But I say it *has been ripping* meeting you in this unexpected way when I thought I was too used up even to want to look at a girl. Tomorrow perhaps——"

"Tomorrow we are returning to London on the early morning train." Nona suffered a relapse into her former cold manner. She was a democrat, of course, and came from a land which taught that all men were equal. But she was a southern girl and the south had been living a good many years on the thought of its old families after their wealth had been taken away. Therefore, there were limits as to what degree of friendliness, even of familiarity, one could endure from a gardener's son.

Nevertheless, the young fellow was a soldier and, one felt instinctively, a gallant one.

"Good-by; I hope you may soon be quite well again," Nona added, and then went across the grass to the gardener's house.

The young man was not accustomed to the poetic fancies that had been besetting him this last quarter of an hour; they must be due to weakness. But somehow the strange girl looked to him like a pale ray of afternoon sunshine as he watched her disappear. She did not come near his resting place again.

CHAPTER IX
"But Yet a Woman"

M ost of the next day the American Red Cross girls devoted to seeing London. They had visited The Tower and Westminster Abbey and the Houses of Parliament soon after their arrival. So, as the sun was shining with unusual vigor for London, they concluded to spend the greater part of their final time out of doors.

London in late May or early June is a city transformed. During the winter she is gray and cold and formidable, so that the ordinary American traveler often finds himself antagonistic and depressed. Then the Englishman appears as cold and unfriendly as his skies. But let the sun shine and the flowers bloom in the parks and the spirit of the city and its people changes.

Naturally, on account of the shadow of the war, the Red Cross girls had anticipated an atmosphere of sorrow and gloom over London. But to their utter amazement on the surface of things there was no such effect. There were, of course, many families in grief over the passing of one of their dearest, or in even more tragic anxiety over the fate of others either at the front or prisoners of war. But whatever the private suffering, there was slight sign of it. No one was wearing mourning, the theaters and restaurants seemed to be doing a good business and the streets and parks were everywhere crowded.

Except that the flags of the Allied Nations waved from nearly every public building and large shop, and that the taxicabs carried placards urging men to enlist, there was little to suggest a nation at war.

Yes, there was one other curious sight which Barbara from the top of an omnibus discovered. Over the roofs of the important government buildings and above many of the great private houses hung a kind of flat screen of heavy wire netting, closely woven. From a distance it formed a cobweb effect, as though gigantic spiders had been spreading their great webs over London.

"I wonder what that means?" asked Barbara, pointing upward, and then knew the answer, although she listened politely while Mildred explained.

"Oh, the wire is to prevent bombs from dropping down on the house tops when London has her great Zeppelin raid. Father began telling me that London must expect them to occur as soon as the war broke out."

Nona, who had been looking pensive, now leaned over from the back seat where she was sitting with Eugenia.

"I am not wishing any harm to London; I adore it. But if the Germans are going to send their marvelous army of the air to bombard the city, don't you wish it would happen while we are here?"

Barbara laughed, Mildred shook her head and Eugenia said seriously:

"Nona, you don't look in the least like a bloodthirsty person. I can't understand you, child. You talk as if you had no sense of fear and I have not been able to make up my mind whether it is because you know nothing of danger or whether you are different from most women. But remember that we are going to our work tomorrow, and I don't think there will be many of the horrors of this war that we shall miss seeing. I am afraid I am a coward, for I dread a great part of them. But isn't that the hospital we are looking for? At least, it will be a tremendous inspiration to meet the woman who has done more for nursing among the British soldiers than any other woman in this war. Dr. Garrett Anderson established the first woman's hospital at Claridge's Hotel in Paris a month after the war broke out, together with Dr. Flora Murray. And the women have done such wonderful surgical work that all the country is talking about them."

Barbara whistled softly. "So they brought this Dr. Anderson back to London and made her a major, the first woman ever given military rank in the British Army!" she exclaimed. "When one considers the Englishman believes 'a woman's place is the home,' it is hard to tell how he is going to reconcile what women are doing to help in this war, men's work as well as their own. But I'll bet you the English won't give the women the vote when the war is over, just the same. They can go back home then, although a good many of the poor things won't have any homes to go to."

Eugenia revealed an annoyed frown. She was doing her best to find good in Barbara Meade, her New England conscience assured her there must be good in everybody. But so far Barbara's trying qualities were much more conspicuous.

"I do wish that you would not use slang, Barbara," she urged almost plaintively. "It may be all right in the west, but really it will give English people such an unfortunate impression of us."

Barbara flushed. Of course she must break herself of this habit; nevertheless, she would like to have mentioned that she had heard a good deal of slang since arriving in England and although unlike the American kind, equally amusing. However, as it was now time to dismount from the top of their bus, this required all her energy and intelligence.

The meeting with Dr. Louise Garrett Anderson was necessarily brief, the distinguished woman happening to have a single free hour had consented to meet the new nurses and wish them God-speed. But the visit to the hospital was also important, because the American Red Cross girls were to have tea with the other nurses who were to accompany them across the Channel the next morning.

The new hospital just back of the British trenches at NeuveChapelle had sent a hurried call to London for more assistance and the four American girls and four British girls were to make the journey immediately.

Crossing the hall to the dining room, Barbara just had time to whisper to Mildred:

"I have a dreadful premonition that I am not going to be popular with English nurses. When you consider how 'New England' feels toward me, what can you expect of England?" and Barbara made a wry face behind Eugenia's back, wishing for the nine hundred and ninety-ninth time in her life that she only looked larger and older and more important.

The meeting of the girls was not very successful. It may be that they were all shy and that they really wished to be friendly without knowing how to approach each other. But this certainly did not appear to be true. For after they were properly introduced by the superintendent of the hospital, the English girls nodded, said "how do you do?" and then sat down again and continued talking to one another, as if the Americans had vanished as soon as their names were spoken.

It was embarrassing. Barbara was angry; nevertheless, her sense of humor made her feel an inclination to giggle. Mildred Thornton seemed distressed and awkward; one could tell from her expression that she was once more feeling her old lack of social graces. She was under the impression that it must be her duty to make things more comfortable without in the least knowing how. Eugenia was simply returning a New England manner to the land whence it came, while Nona Davis was frankly puzzled by the situation.

All her life she had been taught that one's first duty was to make a stranger feel welcome in one's own land. The well-bred southern man or woman will straightway cease to talk of his own affairs to become interested in a newcomer's. They wish to make the stranger happy and at home and in the center of things. But this did not seem to be true of this particular party of English girls. Nona wondered why they should be so unlike the other English people they had been meeting. Perhaps they were rude because they belonged to a class of society that knew no better. You see, Nona's feeling for "family" was very strong. She was to learn better in the days to follow, learn that it is the man or woman who counts, and not who his grandmother or grandfather chanced to be; but the lesson was still before her.

She was now studying the four other girls, too interested to be annoyed by their manners, and yet conscious of the antagonism that they seemed to feel.

However, the four English girls were not in the least alike, which was one reason for their attitude. Two of them appeared in awe of the third, while the fourth girl silently watched the others. The most important girl was extremely tall, had fair hair, a large nose and a lovely English complexion. She was the Honorable Dorothy Mathers. The second was the daughter of a farmer, healthy and in a way handsome. If strength alone counted she would be the best of the nurses. Her name was Mary Brinton and she spoke with a broad Yorkshire dialect, but hardly said anything except "My Lady this, and my Lady that" and was evidently not accustomed to titled society. The third girl was from London, a doctor's daughter and a friend of Lady Dorothy's, Daisy Redmond, while the fourth, whose name was Alexina McIntyre, had given no clue to her history.

However, she it was who finally forced the group of eight girls to betray a mild human interest in one another.

She had reddish hair, freckles on her nose, wore glasses, had a delightful mouth, large, with fine white teeth.

She happened to be gazing directly at Barbara when she first spoke, but her voice was uncommonly loud, so that it forced everybody's attention.

"Please, you little wee thing," she said, "tell us whatever made you come over the ocean to help with our war nursing? Did you think we hadn't enough nurses of our own, that we needed babies like you?"

Barbara stiffened. She had half an idea of declaring that she for one intended going back home at once. Then to her relief she discovered that her questioner had not intended being unkind. There was a sudden twinkle in her light-blue eyes, as if she had become aware of the discomfort in the atmosphere and wished to relieve it by a frivolous speech.

"I'm Scotch," she added with a charming burr in her accent. "I said that to wake you up."

Then Barbara smiled back again and afterwards sighed, "Oh, I am used to having that remark made to me." She looked steadfastly across the space of carpet dividing the eight girls. "The sheep from the goats," she thought to herself. Aloud she merely said:

"I hope with all my heart that in spite of my being so small you are going to find me, and indeed all of us, useful. If you don't, you know, we can go back. But we used to have a saying in our hospital, out in Nebraska, that sometimes brains succeed best in nursing as in other things, rather than brawn."

Only the Scotch woman understood her meaning. However, the ice being broken, afterwards there was an attempt at conversation, until finally in desperation Eugenia gave the signal for farewells.

"We shall meet again in the morning," she said at parting, but showing no enthusiasm at the prospect.

"I am sorry," Mildred Thornton remarked, once the four girls were back again in their lodgings, "but I am afraid for some reason the girls we have just met feel a prejudice against our nursing in the same hospital with them. I wonder what they could have heard against us? Everyone else has been so grateful and kind. I hope they won't make the work harder for us. All of us except Eugenia are inexperienced."

Eugenia nodded her head in agreement. "I am afraid the girl they called Lady Dorothy did not seem to favor us. It is a pity, because she is related to a great many important people, I'm told. But never mind, even if she does dislike us, she can't interfere with our doing good work."

Curled up on the bed, Barbara yawned. "Oh, don't let us look for trouble. One of the things we have got to expect is that some of the English nurses won't like our American ways or our methods of nursing. We have just to remember that we came over here to preach the gospel of peace, not war, and not dislike anyone. Well, our real life work begins tomorrow. Then we will see what stuff we are made of. I am glad our hospital is partly supported by American money and that Mrs. Payne of New York is sometimes in charge of things. I haven't yet become an Anglomaniac; so far I only love the soldiers."

The next morning the trip to the coast followed, and thence across the Channel the way was strangely uneventful. Except that the four American girls now wore their Red Cross costumes, they might have been taken for four girls on a spring shopping journey to Paris. The Channel boats were crossing and recrossing from England to France and back again just as if they had no enemies in the world.

However, the men guiding the destinies of the little steamers were under no such impression. Every foot of the way was traveled with infinite caution. For at any moment disaster might overtake them from the sea or air. But there was no German bomb to destroy the shimmering gold of the atmosphere this May morning, nor dangers in the pathway through the sea. Moreover, from tall towers along both coasts farseeing eyes were watching and protecting the passage of the Channel boats. This morning some of them were carrying passengers across, others khaki-clad soldiers to relieve their wounded comrades.

One surprise, however, awaited the American girls. Quite unexpectedly they discovered that Mrs. Curtis and her son were also crossing the Channel to France on their boat. And Mrs. Curtis reported that Lady Dorian had been taken to The Tower in London where she was being held as a political spy.

CHAPTER X
Behind the Firing Lines

I t was about seven o'clock in the morning ten days later.

Over green fields the sun was shining and the birds were singing in the tops of the tall chestnut trees which were now covered with fragrant blossoms. These trees stood close about an old mansion which was enclosed by a high stone wall with no opening save a tall iron gate connecting with the avenue that led in a straight line to the house. But although there was a small lodge beside it, the gate stood open.

The old stone house itself was strangely built. It had three towers, one taller than the rest, commanding a sweeping view of the country near by. At one side of the building an old stone cloister led to a small chapel a few hundred yards away. And this morning two girls were walking quietly up and down this cloister in uniforms not strikingly unlike those that used long ago to be worn by the young demoiselles of the ancient "Convent of the Sacred Heart" in northern France. But these two modern girls belonged to a newer and braver sisterhood, the order of the Red Cross.

They were Barbara Meade and Nona Davis, but their faces suggested that years, not days, must have passed over them. Their cheeks were white, their expressions strained. From Barbara's eyes and mouth the suggestion of sudden, spontaneous laughter had disappeared. She looked a little sick and a little frightened.

Nona was different, although she suggested a piece of marble. The experiences of the past ten days had brought out the fighting qualities in this young southern girl. Her golden-brown eyes were steady, she carried her chin up and her shoulders straight. She looked the daughter of a soldier.

Now she put her arm across the smaller girl's shoulder.

"Let us go for a walk," she suggested. "No one in the hospital wants our services for a while and breakfast won't be served for another hour. It will do you good to get away from the thought of suffering. We need not go far; besides, the country near here is entirely peaceful."

Barbara said nothing in reply, but taking her consent for granted, the two girls left the cloister and went down the avenue to the open gate and so out into the countryside.

They did not seem to feel like talking a great deal; the endless chatter that had kept them busy during the trip across had died away. But the morning was lovely and the countryside so peaceful that the thought of the scene of battle not far off seemed almost incredible. They were in the midst of a meadow and orchard country of rolling level fields. Beyond them, however, was a line of hills and a forest. But there were no other large houses near, only some small cottages at the edges of the meadows. These belonged to the French peasants, and although the men were now in the trenches, still they appeared thrifty and well kept. For so far, though the enemy watched so near, this part of the country had escaped the actual warfare. The hospital was only a bare five miles from the British line of soldiers, yet was comparatively safe. And for this reason the famous old French school had been emptied of its pupils and turned over to the Red Cross.

As they left the big gate Nona glanced behind her. From the top of the tallest tower floated a white flag, the emblem of peace, and yet bearing upon it a cross of red, symbol of suffering. Then just for an instant the thought crossed her mind, Would this flag continue to protect them throughout the war?

But as there was no possible answer to this question she turned once more to the idea of diverting her companion.

Barbara did not seem to be noticing anything. She was downcast and wandered along with her eyes fixed upon the ground.

"I do not think you ought to worry so or take your breakdown so seriously, Barbara," Nona began. "Why, it might have happened to any one in the world and only shows how keenly you feel things. Next time you will be better prepared."

But the other girl shook her head. "I had no right to come to Europe to help with the Red Cross nursing if I haven't nerve enough not to flunk. Think of it, Nona, the very first time I was called upon to give assistance of real importance, to faint!" The girl's voice expressed the limit of self-contempt. "And this when Eugenia and Lady Mathers were the two other nurses. I would almost rather have died than have had it happen. I believe Eugenia had to stop and drag me out of the surgeon's way. But she has been very kind since, and after all my brave talk on the steamer has not yet mentioned my downfall. I suppose I ought to go home and carry out my threat."

The tears were sliding down Barbara's cheeks, but in spite of this Nona smiled.

"You are the last person in the world to play quitter," she returned quietly. "Now look here, Barbara, you and I know that since we arrived at the hospital we have both been feeling that perhaps we were not wanted and that all our efforts and dreams of helping are going to amount to little." She stopped and for a moment laid both hands on her friend's shoulders. "Well, let's you and I show people differently. I haven't had much experience and so I am perfectly willing to help in any way I can be useful until I learn more. You know you went to pieces the other day, not because you did not have courage to help, but because you have been seeing so many horrors all at once and you have not yet gotten used to them. That poor fellow———"

But Barbara's eyes were imploring her friend to silence. "Let's don't talk about him any more," she begged. "I was used up, there had been so many others and then this soldier somehow reminded me of some one I knew."

Barbara drew a deep breath and squared her shoulders. It may be that the thought of the some one had given her new resolution. "Of course, you know I mean to keep on trying," she added finally.

Then taking off her nurse's cap and flinging back her head, the girl called to Nona, "Catch up with me if you like; I am going to run. It always makes me feel better when I've been having the blues." And the next instant she had turned off from the road along which they had been walking and was flying across one of the meadows as swiftly as a child chasing butterflies.

Just at first Nona attempted running after her. She too wanted to feel the blood racing in her veins and the wind fanning her cheeks. But her companion's flight was too swift. Nona slowed down and followed more quietly.

What an odd girl Barbara Meade was and what a queer combination of childishness and cleverness! Assuredly she had not succeeded in making herself popular at the hospital to which they had lately come. Probably Nona understood more of the situation than Barbara. Already for some reason there had been talk of asking the younger girl to go back to London, if not to her own home. Nona wondered if this were due to Barbara's appearance or her manner. Surely her single failure should not have counted so seriously against her, unless there were other reasons. Nevertheless, she herself believed in her and meant to stand by until Barbara had her chance.

Barbara had ceased running now, and as Nona approached her dropped down on her knees. She had come to the end of the meadow down the slope of a hill and everywhere around the earth was covered with violets.

In a few moments her hands were full of them. "We will take these back to the hospital," she said as cheerfully as though she never had a moment of depression. "I have promised to read to two of the soldiers who are better. They say it amuses them, I have such a funny American voice."

The next minute she was up and off again, this time with her arm linked inside Nona's. "There is such a dear little French house over there. Let's go and see who lives in it now that we are so near."

Nona glanced at her watch. It was a man's watch and had once belonged to her father.

"I have a delightful scheme. It isn't yet eight o'clock and neither you nor I have to go on duty until ten. Ever since we arrived I have wanted to see inside one of these little French huts. So if the people who live in this one are friendly let's ask them to give us coffee and rolls. I can talk to them in French and explain where we come from, then later perhaps we can walk on a little further."

The girls were now within ten yards of the cottage. No one was outdoors, yet there were noises on the inside and through the one small stone chimney the smoke poured out into the air, bringing with it a delicious odor of coffee. Nevertheless, the two girls hesitated. They had been told that the French peasants were always courteous to strangers, and yet it might be difficult to explain their errand.

But they were spared the trouble, for at this instant the heavy wooden door was pushed open and a woman stepped out into the yard.

But after the first glance the two girls stared, not at the woman, but at each other.

"It can't be," Barbara murmured weakly. "I am not seeing things straight."

"Unfortunately, I'm afraid you are," Nona answered, and keeping tight hold of Barbara drew her forward.

"Good morning, Mrs. Curtis," she exclaimed. "I was under the impression that you were in Paris. It seems more than strange for us to run across each other again and you so near the hospital where we have been located."

At Nona's words Mrs. Curtis at once came forward and held out both hands. She was wearing a kimono and did not look attractive, but she smiled so kindly that at least Barbara relented.

"I don't wonder at your surprise," she returned immediately. "Only I happen to have the advantage of already knowing what had become of you four girls. But my being near is not so strange as you may think. I told you my son wanted to see what is taking place inside the British trenches. We had to go to Paris for certain papers we could not get in London. But the firing line at present is only a few miles from here, as you know. So, as I wanted to be reasonably near and still in no danger, my son and I looked about to find some place where I could live. There is only an old woman here and a half-witted son. The father and sons are at the front, of course. But I don't mind being uncomfortable, and then knowing the hospital was so near was such a comfort both to my son and me."

Mrs. Curtis had not ceased talking an instant and seemed to expect no reply. "Won't you come in and have coffee with me now?" she urged. "The house is clean as a pin and I've a letter from my son to Mildred Thornton I should be so much obliged if you would take to her. I was going to walk over with it myself some time today, but I did not know whether an outsider would be allowed to enter the hospital. One can't guess what the restrictions may be in these war times."

She led the way and both girls followed, Barbara because she very much wanted the coffee and to see inside the little French house. She was annoyed at the thought of Brooks Curtis writing to Mildred so soon, but it was scarcely any business of hers. In any case, she did not see how she could prevent it, since Mrs. Curtis would undoubtedly deliver her son's letter unless one of them did.

Nona, however, had no such feeling. She simply had a half-conscious prejudice against breaking bread with a woman whom she neither liked nor trusted. But then she had no real reason for her point of view and had promised herself to rise above it.

Of course, it might be only a coincidence, Mrs. Curtis' evident intention to attach herself to them. But after all, what possible reason could she have except the desire for a little friendly intimacy? Naturally she must be lonely with her son away on his newspaper work.

CHAPTER XI
Out of a Clear Sky

T he girls remained longer than they expected in the little hut. It was extraordinarily interesting, with a thriftiness and tidiness that were characteristically French. Indeed, living seemed to have been reduced to the simplest conditions.

One big room formed the center of the hut. It had a stone floor and a big fireplace where the food was cooked over a peat fire. A plain wooden table and some benches were the only furniture, except two tall and strangely handsome chairs, which must have been the property of some old French family. They had drifted into the cottage by mistake, probably as a gift to an old servant.

On the walls of the room hung a gun of a pattern of the Franco-Prussian war, a cheap lithograph of President Poincairé, and one of General Joffre and General French. So this little hut was also filled with the war spirit. But the old French *mère* explained that her husband and four sons were in the battle line, so few persons had a greater right to a display of patriotism.

The two American girls found the old French woman one of the most picturesque figures they had ever imagined. She wore a bodice and short blue cotton skirt and a cap with pointed ends. Her shoes were wooden and her stockings homespun. Although only between fifty and sixty years old, her visitors were under the impression that Mère Marie must be at least seventy except for her vigor. For her shoulders were bent and her tanned cheeks wrinkled into a criss-cross of lines. Only her black eyes shone keenly above a high arched nose, and she moved with a sprightliness any young person might envy.

Then too she was agreeably hospitable to her unexpected guests, though not communicative. She did not appear to wish to talk about her own affairs.

But although the old woman was so interesting, her son Anton was a dreadful person of whom the two visitors felt a little afraid. He was almost uncanny, like a character you may have seen in a play, or read of in some fantastic book. His coarse black hair hung down to his shoulders and was chopped off at the end in an uneven fashion, his eyes were black and stared, but with a peculiar blank look in them, and his big mouth hung open showing huge yellow teeth. One of the unhappy things about the boy was that he looked so like the woman who was his mother and yet so horribly unlike her because there was no intelligence behind the mask of his face. He did not look brutish, however, only vacant and foolish, and sat in the corner mumbling to himself while Nona and Barbara and Mrs. Curtis had their coffee and rolls.

But once the two girls were away from the little house, Barbara, glancing behind, saw the boy following them. First she shook her head at him, pointing toward his own home, then she brandished a stick. The lad only grinned and kept after them.

The girls had not yet started back to the hospital, as they had more than an hour before them and the morning was too beautiful to be wasted.

"We have got to get rid of that boy somehow, Nona; he gives me the creeps," Barbara suggested. "Suppose we slip out of this field, which may belong to them, and go down to the foot of that little hill. There is an orchard on the other side of the wall and we can stay there under the trees until we must go back to work. Hope no one will think it wrong, our having wandered off in this fashion! The truth is they will probably be too busy to miss us. At least, I am glad that Mildred and Eugenia are being so successful. They may save the day for the United States until our chance comes."

The two girls then sat down in the grass under an old French apple tree, which looked very like one of any other nationality, but was the more romantic for being French. This country of northern France ravaged by mad armies is an orchard and vineyard land and one of the fairest places on earth.

Looking up into the clear sky, Nona spoke first.

"It is as though the war were a horrible nightmare, isn't it?" she began, leaning her chin on her hand and gazing out over the country. "But do you know, Barbara, dreadful as you may think it of me, I am not content to stay on here in the shelter of the hospital, hard and sad as the work of caring for the wounded is. I feel I must know what the battlefield is like, smell the smoke, see the trenches. Often I think I can hear the booming of the great guns, see the wounded alone and needing help before help can come. I am going over there some day, though I don't know just how or when I can manage it."

The girl's face was quiet and determined. She was not excited; it was as if she felt a more definite work calling her and wished to answer it.

Then Nona quieted down, and without replying Barbara lay resting her head in the older girl's lap. There was a growing sympathy between them, although so unlike.

Barbara's blue eyes were upturned toward the clear sky when suddenly her companion felt her body stiffen. For an instant she lay rigid, the next she pointed upward.

"Nona," she exclaimed in a stifled voice, "it doesn't seem possible, but— well, what is that in the sky over there? Perhaps we are not so far from the fighting as you believe."

Nona followed the other girl's gaze, but perhaps she was less far-sighted and her golden brown eyes had not the vision of her friend's blue ones.

"Why, dear, I only see two small black clouds." Then she laughed. "We are talking like Sister Anne and Bluebeard's wife. Remember Sister Anne's speech. 'I can only behold a cloud of dust arising in the distance.'" And Nona made a screen of her hand, laughingly placing it over her eyes.

But Barbara jumped to her feet. "Don't be a goose, Nona. Look, I am in earnest. Those are not clouds, they are aeroplanes and I believe they are trying to destroy each other."

But there was no need now for Barbara to argue; the situation was explaining itself.

Even in this brief moment of time the two air-craft had come closer, the one plainly in pursuit of the other. But they made no direct flight. Now and then they both hung poised in the air, then they darted at each other, or one plunged toward the earth and the other soared higher.

"One of them must be a German scout trying to locate the enemy's position near here," Barbara remarked. She herself a few weeks before would not have believed that she could have seen such a spectacle as the present one without being overpowered with alarm and excitement. But war brings strange changes in one's personality. Both girls were entranced, awed, but above all profoundly interested. They had not yet thought of fear for themselves nor for the men who must be guiding the destinies of the ill-omened birds now driving nearer and nearer toward them. But for the moment one could not associate human beings with these winged creatures; they were too swift and terrible.

The German plane was evidently the larger and heavier of the two.

It could escape only by disabling the other craft, but the smaller one would not remain long enough in one position to have the other's guns turned upon it.

Now and then there were reports of explosions in the air above them. Nona and Barbara expected to see one or the other of the two machines disabled, but somehow the shots missed their aim.

Barbara had a sudden remembrance of having once seen a fish-hawk chased by a kingfisher. The resemblance was strange. Here was the great bird, powerful and evil, moving heavily through the air, while the smaller one darted at it, now forward, now backward, then to the side, causing it endless annoyance, even terror. Yet the larger bird could not move swiftly enough to be avenged.

Once the two planes circled almost out of sight and unconsciously the two watchers sighed, partly from relief, although there was a measure of disappointment. For whatever terror the spectacle held was overbalanced with wonder. Moreover, by this time they were both becoming exhausted. Nona started to sit down again to rest her eyes for a moment.

The next instant Barbara clutched her. Back into their near horizon the fighting air-craft reappeared, and now it was plain enough that the larger was swaying uncertainly. The smaller aeroplane made a final dash toward it, another report sounded, then a white flash appeared and afterwards a cloud of heavy yellow smoke. Away from the smoke, still lumbering uncertainly but keeping a course in the desired direction, the big Taube machine was sailing out of sight. For a few moments longer the smaller aeroplane hung suspended, although it was impossible to see more than the outline of its great white wings through the thick vapor surrounding it.

Then the wings began to waver and the aeroplane to descend toward the earth.

Instinctively, with almost the same emotion that a child feels in reaching the scene a falling balloon, Nona and Barbara ran forward. Unless its course changed the aeroplane must fall in a field not more than two hundred yards away.

But the atmosphere about them, which a short while before had been clear and fragrant, was now growing stifling, and blowing about them was a yellow cloud.

With a suffocating sensation Nona put up her hand to her throat. What could be the trouble with her? She could see Barbara running on ahead, and the great ship fluttering downward, leaving much of the cloud of smoke dissolving behind it. Once she tried to call to her companion, but the feeling of choking was too painful. It would make no difference if she should sit down for a few moments. If there were any service to be done a little later when this curious sensation had passed she could go on.

But whatever the poisonous air that had suddenly come out of the blue heavens the fumes grew thicker on the ground. No sooner had she sat down than Nona dropped backward, her mouth opening slightly and her face turning a queer dark color.

Nevertheless Barbara kept on. From the beginning she had been slightly in advance of Nona and running more quickly. She had been conscious of the sudden thickening of the atmosphere, but had put up her hand, covering her nose and mouth and so had gotten away from the fumes. Moreover, she had not become aware that Nona was not following. Naturally the sight ahead held her mind and eyes.

The airship as it drew nearer the earth seemed to hold its wings outspread, quiet as a weary bird settling to rest. The machinery did not appear to have been seriously wrecked by whatever bomb its enemy had finally used. Barbara could by this time plainly see a man still seated at his post, his hand holding his steering gear. Yet the man looked not like a man so much as a wooden image and seemed unaware of what he was doing. The instant his machine touched the earth he fell forward face downward, rolled over a little when one of the giant wings of his air-craft partly covered him.

CHAPTER XII
First Aid

As soon as Barbara reached the scene of the wreck she turned to seek Nona's advice and aid. But to her amazement there was no evidence of her companion. Stupidly she continued to stare. It was impossible to conceive what could have become of Nona, yet the last quarter of an hour had been so full of strange happenings that there was small wonder at Barbara's bewilderment.

A moment later, a few yards from where they had first begun to run, she saw Nona's figure lying in a crumpled heap upon the ground. Yet was it imaginable that this could be Nona? Had she fainted or stumbled? The recollection of the suffocating gas about them really did not occur to Barbara, as she had felt its effects so slightly.

Yet here she stood torn between two duties. Should she return and find out what had happened to her friend or try first to release the man?

Barbara suffered only a brief indecision. Though she may have failed in her first week's work at the hospital, her training as a nurse now asserted itself. And one of the supreme requisites of the successful nurse is that she use her judgment without unnecessary delay.

Straightway Barbara attempted dragging the unconscious man from his seat in the wrecked aeroplane, it being, of course, out of the question to move the machine itself. But the body felt as heavy and inert as if there were no life inside. Still she tugged, and though so miniature a person her muscles and nerves were for the time at least strong and steady.

The man was tall, an Englishman Barbara guessed him to be, but happily he was thin. Many months devoted to war's service leaves little flesh upon a soldier, and these modern soldiers of the air bear perhaps the most terrific strain of all.

But once the man's head was in the open air Barbara knelt beside him. So far as she could discover he did not appear to be wounded; there was no blood upon him anywhere. Holding her smelling salts under his nose, he showed no sign of consciousness. Then she worked his arms back and forth, so as to stimulate the action of the heart, used every first aid method that her three years of study had taught her. This case was unlike any she had ever known. As she worked an idea came to Barbara. Once she recalled a man having been brought into the hospital overcome by the fumes of gas.

Such a possibility was absurd with this case and yet the face had the same dark, frightful look.

Nevertheless, Barbara Meade was not in the least hopeless, nor did she for an instant cease to work, though now and then she was forced to glance toward the spot where Nona remained so quiet. What could be the matter? Why did she not come to her aid?

All this, of course, took place in a very few minutes. A little later when Barbara gave another frightened look across the fields, she discovered that Nona had gotten up and was walking toward her. She seemed dizzy and uncertain, but there was evidently nothing serious the matter.

Moreover, there was no time for inquiries, for just as Nona reached her, Barbara's patient stirred, coughed and struggled to regain his breath. Then for the first time the nurse put her arm about her friend. The air would do more for the stupefied man than she could.

Soon after he opened his eyes and in an incredibly short time pulled himself out from beneath his aeroplane. He then stared in a dazed half-blind fashion at the two girls standing near him in nurses' uniforms, in the center of a ploughed field.

But war admits of no surprises. Only the two American Red Cross girls had not yet grown accustomed to the possible strangeness of their adventures. Moreover, they were frightened at the appearance of their first hero. He was not in the least what one would expect an aviator to be. This man was not young according to Nona's or Barbara's ideas. He must have been about thirty, his hair and eyes were dark and the lines of his face stern and severe. His skin was now a queer mottled color, with ugly blue splotches.

However, he began struggling to speak. But his tongue was so swollen that he choked and coughed, neither did he seem able to see clearly.

Meanwhile Nona Davis, although considerably less affected, was also plainly not herself. She too coughed uncomfortably and seemed weak and stupid. She expressed no surprise over what had just taken place and offered her friend neither advice nor assistance. But Barbara had already made up her mind. They must get back to the hospital and as soon as possible. Yet her patient could not walk, Nona could not help, and Barbara did not wish to leave them while she went for assistance.

Fortunately, however, in looking about she discovered that Anton, the boy whom they had been endeavoring to escape, had been attracted by the vision in the air. Or if he had not seen it, he was now plainly visible not far away, staring in a bold, half-terrified fashion at the scene, which was past his understanding.

Barbara summoned him imperatively.

Between them they then managed to get the air man clear of his machine. As soon as he was on his feet, with Anton's and Barbara's arms grasping his, he stumbled on for a few steps. Afterwards he found himself better able to walk.

"Extraordinary thing," he began, and Barbara immediately thought his words and manner so intensely English that she wanted to laugh. Would any American man under the same circumstances remain so coldly dignified and superior as this one appeared?

"I am not in the least hurt, you know, only confoundedly weak and suffocated," he said finally. "New trick, that of our enemy's; they have been using their asphyxiating gas on our soldiers in the trenches, but this is the first time a gas bomb has been thrown from a Taube aeroplane. Lucky thing for me the gas was too heavy to stay long in the upper air."

This speech was made thickly and with a great deal of effort, but both Nona and Barbara were able to understand. They knew, of course, of the use of the chlorine missiles, Germany's novel weapon of war, which had lately been thrown into the trenches of the Allies. The papers had been full of the mysterious effects the gas had upon the soldiers. How stupid not to have dreamed of this! Of course, the situation was now explained, even Nona's odd share in it. Evidently the poisonous gas which they had seen in a greenish yellow cloud encircling the aeroplane had fallen to earth and Nona had been wrapped in its fumes. But it had been too diluted with air to have done her serious harm, and after her fall a favoring wind must have blown it away.

By the time the second field was reached Nona was herself again. Indeed, it was she who decided to hurry on to the hospital and send back aid. They were finding the way too long for the still stupefied man, who could only see dimly and was still suffering as if he had been recently paralyzed.

The two nurses had been missed at the hospital and Nona felt the atmosphere of disfavor as she entered the great stone house.

Fortunately, however, she found their Scotch friend, Alexina McIntyre, waiting in the hall for the arrival of a fresh ambulance of the wounded. The ambulances brought the men from the battle front to this hospital only a few miles away. A few moments later help was dispatched to Barbara.

CHAPTER XIII
The Summons

A few days after Eugenia Peabody opened the door of one of the rooms on the top floor used for the nurses. It was a small room which fortunately the four American Red Cross girls were allowed to share without any of the other nurses. Simple as possible, it contained four cot beds, a single bureau, and a great old-fashioned wardrobe. Convents in France were built long before the days of closets.

Eugenia, looking very exhausted, was like most tired persons, cross, when she discovered Nona and Barbara lying on opposite beds peacefully talking.

However, both girls got up instantly.

"Do try and rest a while, Eugenia," Barbara urged. "You seem dreadfully worn out. Isn't there anything I can do to help you?"

Eugenia dropped down upon the nearest wooden chair shaking her head. And in spite of her weariness the two other girls watched her admiringly. One had to see Eugenia in her nurse's costume to realize what a handsome, almost noble looking girl she was. Her ordinary clothes were so shabby and unbecoming and so old style. But the stiff white cap outlined her broad forehead, her somber dark eyes. Even her too serious and sometimes too severe expression seemed in a measure fitted to the responsibility of her work.

"You are wanted downstairs in the convalescent ward, Nona," she began. "The Superintendent says she finds the things you are able to do very useful, even though you are not trained for the more responsible nursing. But before you go here is a letter that has come from London for you. Who can you know in London, child, to be writing you here?"

Nona was moving toward the door, but she paused long enough to receive her letter and then to stand staring in the stupid fashion people have at the unfamiliar handwriting on the outside.

"I haven't the faintest idea," she answered Eugenia, but tearing apart the envelope she suddenly flushed.

"The letter is from Lady Dorian, Eugenia. Remember we met her on the steamer where she was accused of all kinds of dreadful things. She has been imprisoned in London, but this letter must mean that she is free. Anyhow, I'll tell you what she writes when I come back. I am on duty now and haven't time to wait and read it." This was entirely true. Nevertheless Nona had other reasons for wishing to read her letter alone. Lady Dorian had made a strange impression upon her for so short an acquaintance. She had scarcely confessed it even to herself, but she felt a girl's peculiar hero worship for the older woman. Moreover, she was passionately convinced of her innocence and yet did not wish Barbara or Eugenia to know at once what must be told them afterwards. For Lady Dorian could only have written either to say she had been released or to ask aid. There had been no suggestion of their exchanging letters in their brief acquaintance.

Once Nona was out of the room Barbara inquired:

"What has become of Mildred? Isn't this her afternoon to rest? Nona and I were expecting her in here."

The older girl did not answer; she had gotten up and in spite of her fatigue was walking about the small room. She stopped now and looked out of the tiny casement window.

"Oh, Mildred," she returned carelessly, "has gone to spend the afternoon with that Mrs. Curtis. They are to take a walk somewhere, I think. Mildred said she felt the need of fresh air. I believe Mildred is missing her family more than she likes to confess and this Mrs. Curtis is so kind, Mildred seems pleased to find her living so near us."

On her small cot bed Barbara had managed to get herself into an extraordinary position. She had on her kimono and sat hunched up with her knees in the air and her arms about them while her curly head bobbed up and down like a Chinese mandarin's.

"Sorry," she commented briefly. "I told you on the ship I was afraid Mildred was becoming interested in Brooks Curtis. I don't like Mrs. Curtis locating so near the hospital. Don't see any reason for it except that she and her son do not want to lose sight of Mildred. And it would not surprise me if her son turned up in this neighborhood himself fairly often—oh, to see his mother, of course."

Barbara spoke petulantly, particularly when she discovered that Eugenia was paying scant attention to her remarks.

"Oh, do come on and lie down a while, Eugenia," she concluded. "You behave as if all the Allied forces would go to pieces if you stayed off your job an hour, or at least as if all the soldiers in the hospital would die at once."

Still Eugenia made no reply. Although getting out of her working uniform, she too slipped into a comfortable negligée and letting down her heavy dark hair followed Barbara's rather ungraciously offered advice.

A few minutes later the younger girl stood at the side of her bed with a cup of beef tea in her hands which she had just made over a tiny alcohol lamp.

"Drink this, please, and forgive my bad temper, Eugenia," she murmured. "I presume if I confessed the truth even to myself, I am jealous of your success at the hospital. But honestly I don't think I am being given a fair chance here. Ever since we arrived I have been shoved into the background and never called on for any really important work. Oh, I know I failed that one time, but that is no reason why I shouldn't be all right the next."

While the older girl finished the bouillon Barbara sat down on the side of the bed. Then the moment the cup had been set down, to her surprise Eugenia took hold of her hand almost affectionately.

"You are going to be given a chance, Barbara, at least one that will take a whole lot of courage. It is what I came upstairs to tell you and Nona, and what I have been feeling so worried about. For really I don't know whether you ought to agree. You are both so young and pretty." Eugenia hesitated and Barbara took hold of both her shoulders, giving her a tiny shake.

"What do you mean? I hate suspense worse than anything."

"Oh, simply that four girls have to be appointed for service in the two new motor ambulances that are to bring the wounded soldiers from the battle front to the hospital. The Superintendent has decided to ask you and Nona to take charge of one and Lady Mathers and Daisy Redmond the other. Of course, you can refuse if you like, Barbara, for the work may be dangerous. It isn't that you will have to do very much for the soldiers except to see that they are properly bandaged and keep life in them till you can get them here. Of course there is a surgeon in each ambulance to tell you what to do. The danger is that you will have to go much nearer the fighting line and that you may see even more painful things than you have been seeing in the hospital. Really, child, I don't advise you to attempt it."

For with the first realization of what Eugenia meant Barbara had turned deathly pale and was now fighting a sensation of faintness.

"It isn't that I am in the least afraid, Eugenia," she faltered, as soon as she could trust her voice. Even then it was fairly shaky. "I don't mind running the risk or the work or any of those things. You know what it is, Eugenia; there is no use trying to hide it. I simply haven't the nerve I thought I had. It is seeing the wounded soldiers, so many of them. I lie awake at night and dream the most dreadful dreams. I keep thinking I—but I had better not speak of it. I've simply got to say I can't undertake the work. I hate it too on account of Nona; she is sure to try this ambulance work, for only the other day she told me that she longed to get closer to the scene of action. But what must I say, Eugenia, when I refuse? I'm afraid I can't make any one understand that I'm not exactly a coward; I am used to sickness, but somehow this all seems so different."

Again Eugenia pressed the small hand she held in her large, capable one.

"Tell the truth, my dear, and then go back home to the United States. From the moment I saw you I didn't believe this Red Cross work would be suitable for you. I told you you were too young, and I thought you were too quick-tempered and emotional, though I did not speak of this. There is plenty of nursing you might be able to do at home—children, or old people."

Eugenia was growing sleepy; she had such a little while to rest that she was forgetting to be tactful.

"Whether you wish to go back home or not, Barbara, I'm afraid you must if you won't undertake this ambulance work. The Superintendent says she likes you very much and all that, but really does not feel it wise for you to stay on at the hospital. There is so much nursing required and so little room that the girls who cannot give the best kind of service are really in the way. I am sorry to hurt your feelings, but it is better for me to tell you this than any one else," Eugenia concluded, again made sympathetic by the hurt in the younger girl's face. Barbara looked so broken and humiliated, so intensely ashamed of her own failure. Nevertheless, Eugenia could not help seeing that even at this minute Barbara suggested a little girl who has been caught in wrongdoing at school. She simply did not seem able to appear like a grown-up person into whose hands life and death could be intrusted.

For ten minutes afterwards Barbara made no reply. But she got up and put on her nurse's uniform again, hiding her short brown curls beneath her stiff white cap and covering her blue frock with her white apron bearing its cross of red.

Then for a moment when Eugenia seemed to be asleep Barbara dropped on her knees before the open window, gazing out in the direction where she knew the zone of danger and terror lay. Swiftly the girl uttered a prayer for strength and courage. The next moment she crossed over to Eugenia.

"I am going to undertake the ambulance service. I may flunk that too, but at least I can try, and as the book says, 'angels can do no more.' And I'm distinctly not an angel."

CHAPTER XIV
Colonel Dalton

In the meantime Nona was on duty in the convalescent ward. It was the work that she had been able to attend to with peculiar success ever since her arrival at the base hospital. This was a duty which many of the Red Cross nurses liked the least. For the convalescent soldiers were often like spoiled and nervous children. It was amazing how many drinks of water they required, how frequently their pillows had to be turned, how often letters from home had to be read and re-read until the nurses knew them by heart as well as the patients.

It was a dark, cloudy afternoon when Nona entered the big room and before she had more than crossed the threshold she became aware of an atmosphere of gloom and ill-temper.

Daisy Redmond, the English girl with whom they had crossed the Channel, had been in attendance on the ward before Nona's appearance and she seemed bored and annoyed. She was a very good nurse for an ill person, but too serious and reserved to cheer the convalescent, and on Nona's entrance she gave a sigh of relief.

The room, which was used for the soldiers who were on the high road to recovery from whatever disaster they had suffered, must have been the refectory or the old dining hall of the convent in the days before the Franco-Prussian war. It was an oblong room with a high ceiling crossed by great oak beams. Midway up the walls were of dark oak and the rest of stone. The floor was of stone and the windows high and crossed with small iron bars. While they let in the air and sunlight, it was impossible to see much of the outside world unless one climbed a ladder or chair. Evidently it had been thought best not to permit the little French convent maids to seek for distractions even among the flowers and trees.

So the great room, in spite of its perfect cleanliness, had little suggestion of gayety or beauty to recommend it at present. The floor, walls, beds, everything apparently had been scrubbed to the limit of perfection and were smelling of antiseptics. But there was not a flower in the room, not a picture, only two long rows of beds each containing a weary, impatient soldier, longing to be home with his own people or back at the front with the other Tommies.

Almost anyone might have become discouraged with the prospect of two hours' effort in such surroundings, but Nona never dreamed of flinching.

As she went up toward the first bed, the young fellow with his right arm in a sling who was trying to write with his left hand, used a short word of three letters. He was a boy who worked in a butcher's shop in London. When he saw Nona so near him, he blushed crimson and stammered an apology.

Nona only laughed. "Oh, I say that myself sometimes, inside of me," she whispered. "If it hurts your arm, do let me finish your letter. I'd like to add a line or two anyhow just to let Addie know you are really getting well and not trying to encourage her with false hopes."

The young fellow smiled. It was clever of the little American girl to remember his girl's name. He was glad enough to have her end his letter so that he might lie down again. Besides, he liked to have her sitting near him, she was so pretty—the prettiest nurse in the hospital in his opinion. Five minutes after when Nona had finished his letter and made him comfortable, he sighed to have her leave him. She was only going to another duffer a few beds away, who had been trying to read and dropped all his magazines on the floor. With one of his legs in a plaster cast, he had almost broken his neck trying to fish for them.

So Nona wandered up and down the ward doing whatever was asked of her. She felt that she was being useful in spite of her lack of long experience in nursing. But it was amusing the queer things she was called upon to do.

She was passing one of the cots where a boy lay who had received a wound in his head. He was not more than seventeen or eighteen, and was a blue-eyed, fair-haired boy with a mouth like a young girl's. You would never have dreamed of him as a fighter; indeed, he had left Eton to join the army and had never before known a real hardship in his life. But now a pair of wasted white hands clasped Nona's skirt.

Looking down she discovered that the bandage had slipped off his forehead and that his eyes were full of tears.

Nona's own eyes were dim as she bent toward him.

"Are you suffering again?" she asked gently. "I am so sorry; I thought you were almost well."

"It isn't that," the boy whispered. "I wouldn't mind the pain; it's only—oh, I might as well say it, I want my mother. Funny to behave like a cry-baby. I wish I could sleep. I wonder if you could sing to me?"

At first Nona shook her head. "Why I can't sing, really," she returned. "I have never had a music lesson in my life. I only know two or three songs that I used to sing to my father way down in South Carolina. I expect you hardly know there is such a place."

Then suddenly the boy's disappointed face made the girl hesitate.

She glanced about them. In the bed next to the boy's the man she and Barbara had rescued from the aeroplane disaster lay apparently too deeply absorbed in a bundle of newspapers to pay the least attention to them.

By this time he had almost recovered and was enormously impatient to return to his regiment. It appeared that he was not a regular member of the aviation corps, but a colonel in command of one of the crack line regiments. However, he happened also to be a skilled aviator and on the morning of the accident, having a leave of absence from his command, had gone up to reconnoiter over the enemy's lines.

No, Colonel Dalton would pay no attention to her, Nona felt convinced. He was very quiet and stern and a distinguished soldier, so that most of the nurses were afraid of him.

"If you'll try to sleep, why I'll sing softly just to you, so we need not disturb any one else," Nona murmured, kneeling down by the side of the boy's cot so that her face was not far from his. "I only know some old darkey songs."

Straightway the young English boy closed his eyes. Very quietly in a hushed voice Nona began to sing, believing no one else would listen.

She chanced to be kneeling just under one of the tall windows and the afternoon sun shone down upon her white cap, her pale gold hair and delicate face. If she had known it she was not unlike a little nun, but fortunately Nona had no thought of herself.

She had only a small voice, but it was sweet and clear.

> "All this world am sad and dreary,
>   Everywhere I roam,
> Oh, darkies, how my heart grows weary,
>   Far from the old folks at home."

Not one, but half a dozen soldiers lay quiet listening to Nona's song. She was only aware that the boy for whom she was singing was breathing more evenly as she sang on and that there was a happier curve to his lips. In a few moments more, if nothing occurred to disturb him, he must be asleep.

So Nona did not know that Colonel Dalton, although holding his beloved London newspaper before his face, had been watching her and that her old-fashioned song had touched him.

She was slipping away with her patient finally asleep when he motioned to her.

"It is a wonderful thing you are doing, Miss Davis," he began in a low tone, so as not to disturb the sleeper, "you a young American girl to come over here to help care for our British boys. I want to shake hands with you if I may, you and that clever little friend of yours, who helped me out of my difficulty. I shall be away from the hospital in a few days and back at my post, as I've almost entirely recovered from the effects of the chlorine gas. But later on if I can ever be of service to you in any way, you are to count upon me. I trust that at some future day the English nation can show its appreciation for what the United States has done for us in this tragic war."

Colonel Dalton spoke with so much feeling and dignity that Nona was both pleased and embarrassed. Of course, she seemed like a young girl to him, and yet after all Colonel Dalton could be only a little over thirty. It must be something in his character or in his history that gave his face the expression of sadness and sternness. Although his duties as an officer in the war might already have created the look.

"You are very good," she murmured confusedly. She was moving away when she noticed that Colonel Dalton was staring fixedly, not at her, but at a brooch which she wore fastening her nurse's apron to her dress.

But probably he was in a reverie and not seeing anything at all!

However, Nona did not have to remain long in doubt. Colonel Dalton spoke abruptly.

"That's an extraordinary pin you've got there, a collection of letters isn't it? I wonder if by any chance it represents the motto of your own family?"

Nona shook her head and carelessly unclasped the pin. "No," she answered, "and I have scarcely been able to find out what the letters spell. I wonder if you could tell me."

The man scarcely glanced at the pin. "The letters are 'Vinces,' the Latin for 'Conquer.'" Then strangely enough Colonel Dalton flushed, a curious brick-red, which is a peculiarity of many Englishmen.

"It's a remarkable request I wish to make of you, Miss Davis. But would you mind parting with that little pin? It's an odd fancy of mine, but then every soldier is superstitious and I should like very much to possess it. Possibly because of the meaning of the word, for the word 'Conquer' never meant more in the history of the world than it does to an Englishman today."

But Nona had crimsoned uncomfortably and was clutching at her brooch in a stupid fashion. "I am awfully sorry," she murmured, "it must seem ungracious of me, but I value the pin very much. You see, it was given me by some one——"

"In this country, or in your own?" Colonel Dalton interrupted.

Again Nona hesitated. Suddenly she had become conscious of the unread letter in her pocket which she had just received from Lady Dorian, and of the hour of their parting and her bestowal of the pin.

She smiled. "It wasn't given me in either your country or mine, but upon the sea."

Then she walked over to another patient who required a drink of water.

CHAPTER XV
Newspaper Letters

C uriously Mildred Thornton was also spending an unexpected afternoon. She had been looking forward to her walk with Mrs. Curtis. Mildred too had been feeling the strain of the first weeks at the hospital more than she had confessed. She was one of the girls whom one speaks of as a natural nurse—quiet, sympathetic and efficient—and so had immediately been given especially trying cases. And Mildred was not accustomed to roughing it, since her home surroundings were luxurious and beautiful. So though she had made no complaint and showed no lack of courage, as Barbara had, she was tired and now and then, when she had time to think, homesick.

Mrs. Curtis had been kind and whatever prejudice the other girls felt, she sincerely liked her. Moreover, Mildred also liked her son, although this she had not confessed so freely to herself. But she was thinking of both of them as she walked through the fields to the home of Mère Marie.

Perhaps Mrs. Curtis would have received news from Brooks. He was supposed to be not far away making a study of conditions in the British line of trenches not far from the Belgian border. He must know extraordinarily interesting things. Mildred too shared the almost morbid curiosity which everybody of intelligence feels today. What is a modern battlefield really like, what is the daily life of the soldier, and what is this strange new world of the trenches, where men live and work underground as if all humanity had developed the tendencies of the mole?

Mildred did not share Nona Davis' desire to go and find out these things for herself, but being so near the scene of action as they were could not but stimulate one's interest. And daily the motor ambulances brought the wounded from the nearby battlefield to their door.

At Mère Marie's Mildred first saw the boy Anton sitting crouched before the hut. He leered at her foolishly and said something which she did not understand. So somewhat nervously Mildred knocked on the heavy wooden door. She too was afraid of Anton; one could scarcely help being, although all the people in the neighborhood insisted that he was perfectly harmless. As he used to bring vegetables from his mother's garden and run errands for the staff at the hospital, he was a very well-known character.

However, Mildred was just as glad when the door opened.

But to her surprise, instead of seeing Mrs. Curtis, Brooks Curtis was there to greet her.

He seemed a little nervous at first, but when Mildred showed pleasure at seeing him, became more cheerful.

Mère Marie's big room was empty and so the girl and young man sat down on wooden stools in front of the smouldering peat fire.

It appeared that Brooks was discouraged. So far he had not been allowed to get inside the British firing line and feared that his newspaper at home would be disappointed in him.

Mildred did her best to reassure him. She was accustomed to trying to make people more comfortable. All her life her brother Dick had been confiding his annoyances to her, depending on her sympathy and advice. And Mildred had been missing Dick dreadfully since the first hour of her sailing. For though possibly he was as spoiled and selfish as Barbara Meade plainly thought him, he was a fairly satisfactory brother in his way. So she found it not unpleasant to behave in a sisterly fashion toward Brooks Curtis.

Indeed, half an hour had passed before it occurred to Mildred that Mrs. Curtis had not appeared and that she had not even asked for her.

However, just as she was making up her mind to inquire, Mrs. Curtis came into the room.

She had on a dressing gown and looked pale and ill.

"I am so sorry. I suppose Brooks has explained to you," she began. "But I have a frightful headache and don't feel equal to going out this afternoon. I don't think you should miss your walk, Miss Thornton, you are kept indoors so much at the hospital. So I wonder if you won't take your walk with Brooks instead of me and then come back here and have coffee and cake."

Mildred felt a little uncomfortable. There was no doubt of Mrs. Curtis' illness; seldom had she seen anybody more nervous and wretched from a headache. Yet Mildred did not know exactly what to do or say. Very much she desired to spend a part of her one free afternoon in the air and sunshine away from the pain and sorrow of the hospital. She was not averse to spending it with Brooks Curtis instead of his mother. But she was not sure whether it would be right for her to take a walk alone with a man whom she really knew nothing about. The days on shipboard had made them behave like fairly intimate friends. However, she also felt it would appear stupid and unfriendly of her to refuse. Even if Eugenia and the other girls disapproved later, the whole question of Mrs. Curtis and her son was not their affair. Moreover, Mildred did not intend confiding in them.

So she blushed a little and then answered awkwardly.

"Oh, of course I don't want to miss my walk and I don't mind if Mr. Curtis wishes to come with me. Only he is not to trouble, because I am not afraid to go alone."

Then Mildred felt like stamping her foot. Ever since getting away from the conventional society atmosphere of her own home she had been more at ease and less self-conscious. Had not her friendship with Mrs. Curtis and her son proved that she was not always stiff and silent? Assuredly Brooks had preferred her to any of the other girls, even though they were far prettier and more attractive. Yet here she was, through her old shyness, spoiling everything.

Mildred smiled unexpectedly, which always relieved the plainness of her face.

"I was not telling the truth then," she added, "I should enjoy my walk ever so much more if Mr. Curtis will go with me."

An hour later and the girl and her companion had climbed the nearest hill in that part of the country. It was not quite a mile from the hospital and was not a very high hill, yet Mildred was surprised at the splendid view.

Brooks Curtis had brought with him the fine telescope which he had used on the steamer in spite of the difficulty with his eyes.

He pointed out to Mildred the direction in which General Sir John French's army lay entrenched. One could not see the exact place because the line of trenches covered twelve miles of battle front and many other miles of underground passages. Then he told her that the right wing of the British army which was in position nearest their hospital was under the command of Lieutenant-General Porter and that Colonel Dalton, who was ill, was one of his most talented officers.

Secretly Mildred Thornton was amazed and fascinated. She had been convinced early in their acquaintance that Brooks Curtis was an unusually clever fellow. He was not handsome and there was something a little odd about him. Mildred was sympathetic with people who were not good looking and not at ease. Now she was really surprised at his information about the British army. For after all he had only been in France for a short time.

"But I thought you said you had not been able to go through the trenches," Mildred expostulated, "yet already you know a great deal."

The young man shook his head mournfully. "I know nothing of importance yet," he returned with such emphasis that Mildred was the more impressed. Above all things she admired determination of character.

Then for a few moments neither the girl nor the young man spoke.

Mildred was trying to locate in a vague fashion certain positions of the army which her companion had just described. Two miles farther to the north Mildred could see a low range of hills which seemed deeply curtained by trees. In the midst of those trees Brooks insisted the British army had stationed long-range guns. They were guns of a new character and no one yet knew what their power of destruction might be. Behind the artillery there were telephone connections with the trenches miles away.

Really Mildred Thornton was too interested in the information imparted by her new friend to pay any special attention to what he might be doing.

However, he had taken off his glasses, gotten out a note book and was now writing as rapidly as possible.

By and by he got out an envelope and put the papers inside it, together with some others that were there previously.

At this minute Mildred looked around.

"Oh, dear, it is late; we must be going back as quickly as possible!" she exclaimed, and then got up without allowing her companion opportunity to assist her.

Nevertheless, the young man did not follow her for a moment.

"I wish you would stay just an instant longer," he asked instead.

And when Mildred turned he still held the envelope in his hand.

"I want to ask you a favor, Miss Thornton, and I don't know just how to explain. I wonder if you will be good enough to mail this letter of mine from the hospital along with your own home mail? You see, it is like this with the newspaper fellows, all our mail is so censored that the news we want to send to the United States is usually cut out before it arrives. There is no good my writing exactly what the other fellows send. So I thought if you would mail this for me like private mail along with the nurses' letters, why I'd stand a chance. I know it is asking a good deal of a favor of you. But somehow I have felt you were my friend ever since our first meeting and my mother feels the same way. You see, we are awfully poor. Of course you can't know what that means, but for my mother's sake and my own I'm terribly anxious to make good with my war stories. I feel if I can make a reputation now my future will be assured."

Whether Brooks Curtis was a student of character or not, one does not yet know. But certainly he had gauged Mildred.

If there was anything that did appeal to her it was the thought of another's struggle and the possibility that she might help. Just because she had always spent such a rich and sheltered life her desire to aid others was the stronger. So Mildred promised to mail the letter to an address in Brooklyn, placing the address on the envelope with her own handwriting so as to avoid questioning.

Neither did she feel that she was doing anything unusual. The deception was too small to be considered. Besides, what difference could it make to the hospital authorities if one more letter were added to their mail bag?

"I shall never cease to appreciate your kindness," Brooks Curtis said at parting, "and you won't mind, will you, if now and then Anton brings you other letters to the hospital? I may not be able to get away to bring them myself."

Mildred nodded without thinking of this side of the question seriously. The truth of the matter was that she was in too much of a hurry now to return to her work. Although she had not gone back to Mère Marie's for coffee, they had been out longer than she realized.

CHAPTER XVI
The Ambulance Corps

A few days later it was definitely arranged that Nona Davis, Barbara Meade, Lady Dorothy Mathers and Daisy Redmond should be enrolled in the Red Cross ambulance work.

To understand the service of the Red Cross ambulances one must be familiar with the unusual conditions which existed in this most terrible war of all human history.

Most of us know, of course, that the greater part of the fighting was done at night. By day scouts in aeroplanes endeavored to locate the enemy's positions, while sentries kept guard along the miles of trenches to fire at any man who dared venture within what was called the zone of death. So all the work of war except the actual fighting must take place behind each army's line of entrenchments.

This means that in the early morning, when the night's cruelties were past, the wounded soldiers were carried from the field of battle or from the trenches to some place of safety in the rear. Here nurses and doctors could give them first aid. And this required tremendous personal bravery. The stricken soldiers must be borne in the arms of their companions to the nearest Red Cross, or else lifted into the ambulances or smaller motor cars. These traveled with all possible speed across the tragic fields of the dead, as soon as a lull in the firing made attempt at rescue possible.

There, behind a barricade of trees, or of sand bags, or of a stone wall, or whatever defense human ingenuity could invent, stood white tents, or else a stable or house. These waved flags of white bearing a crimson cross, demanding safety for the suffering.

These temporary hospitals had to be established at any place where the need was greatest. But the soldiers could not remain in these quarters. As soon as possible they were taken to the nearest properly equipped hospital, sometimes fairly near the fighting line. At other times they were loaded into trains and borne many weary miles away.

But in nearly every case they were carried to the cars or to the nearer hospitals in the Red Cross ambulances. They were the only chariots of peace the war had so far acquired.

However, it is good to know that together with all the modern inventions for the destruction of men, science had done all that was possible to make the new Red Cross ambulances havens of comfort and of cure. In Paris, the great Madame Curie, the discoverer of radium, had been giving her time and talent to the equipment of ambulances for the soldiers. From this country much of the money that had been poured so generously into Europe had been devoted to their purchase.

So the four Red Cross girls from the Hospital of the Sacred Heart (so named in honor of the old convent school) were naturally impressed with the importance of their new duties.

The plan was that they were to travel back and forth from the field hospitals with the wounded soldiers who required the most immediate attention. A doctor would be in charge of each ambulance and of necessity the chauffeur. Under the circumstances it was thought better to have two nurses instead of one. The four additional nurses were required because two new ambulances had just been added to the British service, as a gift from New York City, through the efforts of Mrs. Henry Payne, who was especially interested in the Sacred Heart Hospital.

The morning that the girls left for the nearer neighborhood of the battlefield was an exquisite June day. The sun is one of France's many lovers, turning her into "La Belle Dame," the name by which she is known to her own children and to some of her admirers from other lands.

All the nurses who were off duty at the hospital poured out into the garden to say farewell and God-speed to their companions.

Except for the prejudice which Lady Dorothy Mathers and her friends continued to feel against the four Americans, everybody else had been most kind. The English manner is colder than the American or the French, but once having learned to understand and like you, they are the most loyal people in the world.

Three of the American Red Cross girls were beginning to realize this. But Barbara Meade still felt herself misunderstood and disliked. Under normal conditions Barbara was not the type of girl given to posing as "misunderstood" and being sorry for herself in consequence.

The difficulty was that ever since her arrival the horror of the war and the suffering about her had made her unlike herself. She felt terribly western, terribly "gauche," which is the French word meaning left-handed and all that it implies. Then Barbara had a fashion of saying exactly what she thought without reflecting on the time or place. This had gotten her into trouble not once but a dozen times. She did not mean to criticize, only she had the unfortunate habit of thinking out loud. But most of all, Barbara lamented her own failure as a nurse and all that it must argue to her companions. For so far they had the right to consider her a shirker and a coward, or at least as one of the tiresome, foolish women who rush off to care for the wounded in a war because of an emotion and without the sense or the training to be anything but hopelessly in the way.

It was for this reason that Barbara had finally decided to accept the new opportunity offered her. If she should make a failure of it, she agreed with Eugenia's frank statement of her case: she must simply go back home so as not to be a nuisance.

Curious, but one of the reasons why Barbara loathed the thought of her own surrender was the idea that if she turned back, she would have to face Dick Thornton in New York City. This thought had been in her mind all along. For one thing she kept recalling how bravely she had talked to Dick of her own intentions, and of how she had reproached him for his idle existence.

The worst of Barbara's conviction was that should she return a failure, no one would be kinder or more thoughtful of her feelings than Dick. Of course, she had not known him very long, but it had been long enough for her to appreciate that Dick Thornton was utterly without the ugly spirit of "I told you so." But perhaps his sympathy and quiet acceptance of her weakness would be harder to endure than blame.

So it was a very pale and silent Barbara who walked out of the old stone convent that morning with her arm linked inside Eugenia's. She was beginning to appreciate Eugenia more and to realize that her first impression of Miss Barbara Meade's abilities, or lack of them, was not so ridiculously unfair as she had thought.

Certainly no one could be kinder than Eugenia had been in the few days between Barbara's acceptance of her new work and the time for actually beginning it.

She kept looking at her now, feeling almost as one would at the sight of a frightened child. Poor Barbara was pretending to be so brave. Though she had not spoken again of her own qualms, it was plain enough to the older girl that Barbara was almost ill with apprehension. Not that Eugenia believed she was afraid of the actual dangers that might befall her from going so much closer to the battle front. She suffered from the nervous dread of breaking down at the sight of the wounded and so again failing to make good.

The superintendent of the nurses, a splendid middle-aged woman from one of the big London hospitals, was also aware of Barbara Meade's state of mind. For several days with all the other work she had to do she had been quietly watching her. Here at the last moment she had an impulse to tell Barbara to give up. After all, she was such a child and the strain might be too much for her. Then she concluded it would be best to let the girl find out for herself.

The contrast was odd between the two American girls who were answering this new call of war. Nona Davis did not seem nervous or alarmed. Not that she was unconscious either of the dangers or the difficulties. She seemed uplifted by some spiritual emotion. She was like a young Joan of Arc, only she went forth to carry not a sword but a nurse's "Red Badge of Courage."

A little after daylight the four girls and two of the hospital surgeons left for the front. The two new ambulances had been taken directly to the field hospital where they were to meet them.

The night before news had come that there had been fresh fighting and help was needed at once. So one of the hospital automobiles had been requisitioned to transport the little party.

"We will be back by tonight with the wounded," Nona Davis said calmly as she kissed Mildred Thornton good-by. "You are not to worry about us. I don't think we are going into any danger."

Barbara made no attempt at farewells; she simply sat quietly on the back seat of the car with her hand clasped inside Nona's, and her eyes full of tears. Had she tried to talk she might have broken down and she was painfully conscious that the two English girls, Lady Dorothy Mathers and Daisy Redmond, were staring at her in amazement. It was hard to appreciate why if she was afraid of the war nursing, she would not give it up.

The first part of the drive was through country like that surrounding the Sacred Heart Hospital. General Sir John French had given orders that in every place where it was possible the agriculture of France should be respected. The crops must not be trampled down and destroyed, for the rich and poor of France alike must live and also feed their army.

So all along the first part of their route the girls could see women and children at work. They wore the long, dark-blue blouses of the French working classes, at once so much cleaner and more picturesque than the old, half-worn cloth clothes of our own working people.

It was all so serene and sweet that for a little while Nona and Barbara almost forgot their errand.

Then the face of the countryside changed. There were no peasants' huts that were not half in ruins, great houses occupied but a few months before by the wealthy landowners of northern France were now as fallen into disuse as if they had been ancient fortresses. Here and there, where the artillery had swept them, forests of trees had fallen like dead soldiers, and over certain of the fields there was a blight as if they had been devastated with fire.

Then the car brought the little party to the spot where in the morning sunshine they caught the gleam of the Red Cross flag.

The place was a deserted stable sheltered by a rise of ground. To the front lay the British trenches, covered with thatch and the boughs of many trees; to the right and some distance off, hidden behind breastworks, were enormous long distance guns.

Also one of the surgeons explained to Lady Dorothy and Nona, who seemed most interested, that on the hill beyond the hospital where nothing could be seen for the denseness of the shrubbery, several of the officers had their headquarters and from there dictated the operations in the trenches and in the fields.

The night before must have been a busy one, for as the car stopped behind the improvised hospital, soldiers in khaki could be seen staggering back and forth with the wounded, surgeons with their work showing all too realistically upon them. Then there were the sounds as well as the sights of suffering.

As Barbara Meade crawled out of the automobile she felt her knees give way under her and a darkness swallow her up. Then she realized that she must be fainting again.

CHAPTER XVII
Dick

"Steady," a voice said in Barbara Meade's ear, as a strong arm slipped across her shoulders, bracing her upright.

And so surprised was she by the voice and its intonation that she felt herself brought back to consciousness.

"Dick Thornton," she began weakly, and then decided that in truth she must be taking leave of her senses, to have an image of Dick obtrude upon her at such a moment and in such a place.

Naturally curiosity forced her to turn around and so for the instant she forgot herself and her surroundings.

She saw a young man in a khaki uniform of a kind of olive green with a close-fitting cap and visor. But beneath the cap was a face which was like and yet unlike the face of the friend she remembered. This fellow's expression was grave, almost sad, the dark-brown eyes were no longer indifferent and mocking, the upright figure no longer inactive. Indeed, there was action and courage and vigor in every line of the figure and face.

Barbara stepped back a few paces.

"Dick Thornton," she demanded, "have I lost my mind or what has happened? Aren't you several thousand miles away in New York City, or Newport, where ever the place was you intended spending the summer? I simply can't believe my own eyes."

Dick slipped his arm inside Barbara Meade's. For the time no one was noticing them; the scene about them was absorbing every attention.

"Just a moment, please, Barbara, I want to explain the situation to you," Dick asked, and drew the girl away behind the shelter of one of the hospital wagons.

"Sit down for a moment," he urged. "Dear me, Barbara, what have they been doing to you in the few weeks since we said good-by in good old New York? You are as white and tiny as a little tired ghost."

But Barbara shook her head persuasively. "Please don't talk about me," she pleaded. "I must know what has occurred. What could have induced you to come over here where this terrible war is taking place, and what are you doing now you are here? You aren't a soldier, are you?" And there was little in Barbara's expression to suggest that she wished her friend to answer "Yes."

Dick had also taken a seat on the ground alongside Barbara and now quite simply he reached over and took her hand inside his in a friendly strong grasp.

"I don't know which question to answer first, but I'll try and not make a long story. I want you to know and then I want you to tell Mill. I came over to this part of the country so as to be near you. But I haven't wanted to see either of you until I found out whether I was going to amount to anything. If I wasn't of use I was going on back home without making a fuss. You see, Barbara, I suppose your visit to us set me thinking. You had a kind way of suggesting, perhaps without meaning it, that I was a pretty idle, good-for-nothing fellow, not worth my salt, let alone the amount of sugar my father was bestowing on me. Well, I pretended not to mind. Certainly I didn't want a little thing like you to find out you had made an impression on me. Still, things you said rankled. Then you and old Mill went away. I couldn't get either of you out of my mind. It seemed pretty rotten, me staying at home dancing the fox trot and you and Mill over here up against the Lord knows what. So I—I just cleared out and came along too. But there, I didn't mean to talk so much. Whatever is the matter with you, Barbara? You look like you were going to keel over again, just as you did when you tumbled out of that car."

The girl shook her head. "You can't mean, Dick, that you have come over to enlist in this war because of what I said in New York? Oh, dear me, I thought I was unhappy enough. Now if anything happens to you your mother will have every right not to forgive me; besides, I shall never forgive myself."

Barbara said the last few words under her breath. Although hearing them perfectly, Dick Thornton only smiled.

"Oh, I wouldn't take matters as seriously as that," he returned. "I didn't mean to make you responsible for my proceedings. I only meant you waked me up and then, please heaven, I did the rest myself. See here, Barbara, after all I am a man, or at least made in the image of one. And I want to tell you frankly that I've gone into this terrible war game for two reasons. I don't suppose many people do things in this world from unmixed motives. I want to help the Allies; I think they are right and so they have got to win. Then I thought I'd like to prove that I had some of the real stuff in me and wasn't just the little son of a big man. Then, well, here are you and Mill. I'm not a whole lot of use, but I like being around if anything should go wrong. We didn't know each other very long, Barbara, but I'm frank to confess I like you. You seem to me the bravest, most go-ahead girl I ever met, and I am proud to know you. I believe we were meant to be friends. Just see how we have been calling each other by our first names as if we had been doing it always. Funny how we left our titles behind us in New York."

Dick was talking on at random, trying to persuade his companion to a little more cheerfulness. Surely they were meeting again in gruesome surroundings. Yet one must not meet even life's worst tragedies without the courage of occasional laughter.

"But I'm not brave, or any of the things you are kind enough to think me; I'm not even deserving of your friendship, let alone your praise," the girl answered meekly. Her old sparkle and fire appeared gone. Dick Thornton was first amazed and then angry. What had they been doing to his little friend to make her so changed in a few weeks? He said nothing, however, only waited for her to go on.

But Barbara did not continue at once. For of a sudden there was an unexpected noise, a savage roaring and bellowing and then a muffled explosion.

The hand inside the American boy's turned suddenly cold.

"What was that?" she whispered.

But Dick shook his head indifferently. "Oh, just a few big guns letting themselves go. They do that now and then unexpectedly. There is no real fighting. I have been here a week. Sometimes at night there is a steady crack, crack of rifles down miles and miles of the trenches from both sides and as far off as you can hear. Then every once in a while like thunder of angry heathen gods the cannons roar. It's a pretty mad, bad world, Barbara."

By this time the noise had died away and Barbara took her hand from Dick's.

"We must not stay here much longer," she suggested, "yet I must tell you something. You remember all the things I said to you in New York about being useful and a girl having as much courage as a boy and the right to live her own life and all that?"

Dick nodded encouragingly. Nevertheless and in spite of their surroundings he had to pretend to a gravity he did not actually feel. For to him at least Barbara appeared at this moment enchantingly pretty and absurd.

If only she had not been so tiny and her eyes so big and softly blue! Of course, the short brown curls were now hidden under her nurse's cap. But her lips were quivering and the color coming and going in her cheeks, which now held little hollows where the roundness had previously been.

She held her hands tight together across her knees.

"I have turned out a hopeless failure with my nursing, Dick. All the silly things I told you about myself were just vanity. Eugenia and Mildred and even Nona, who has had little experience, are doing splendidly. But the Superintendent and all the people in charge of our hospital want me to go home. You see, the trouble is I'm a coward. Sometimes I don't know whether I am afraid for myself or whether it is because I am so wretched over all the pain around me. I try to believe it is the last, but I don't know. When that cannon was fired I was frightened for us."

Dick Thornton's expression had changed. "Why, of course you were. Who isn't scared to death all the time in such an infernal racket? Suppose you think I haven't been frightened out of my senses all this week? I just go about with my knees shaking and scarcely know what I'm doing. The soldiers tell me they feel the same way when they first get into the firing line; after a while one gets more used to it. But see here, Barbara," Dick's brows knit and the lines about his handsome mouth deepened. "If you feel the way you say you do, in heaven's name tell me what you mean by coming so near the battlefield? Whatever put it into your head to attempt this ambulance work? Why don't you stay at the hospital and make yourself useful? That's what Mildred is doing, isn't she?"

Barbara nodded. "Yes, but I wasn't useful at the hospital. So I decided to walk right up to the cannon's mouth and see if I couldn't conquer myself. If my nerves don't go to pieces here I feel I can endure most anything afterwards." Barbara glanced fearfully about her. Fortunately they were hidden from any sight of suffering. Then she got quietly up on her feet.

"I must go to my work now, I'm afraid I have already been shirking," she said. "But please, Dick, you have not yet answered my question. What is it you are doing with the army? Have you enlisted as a soldier?"

Dick took off his cap. Already his skin had darkened from the week's hardships and exposure, for a line of white showed between his hair and the end of his cap.

"No, I am not a soldier, Barbara. After all, you know I am an American and I don't quite feel like killing anybody, German or no German. So I am trying to do the little I can to help the fellows who are hurt, just as you are, although in a different fashion. Remember I told you once that my real gift might be that of a chauffeur. Well, that's what I am these days, a glorified chauffeur. I am running one of the field ambulances. You see, I am a pretty skilful driver. I go out over the fields with my car whenever the Deutschers give us a chance and with two other fellows pick up the wounded Tommies and try to rush them back to safety. It's a pretty exciting business. But somehow in spite of being scared I like it."

Barbara again held out her hand. "Will you shake hands with me before we have to say good-by? Because I want you to know that when I thought you were careless and good for nothing you were really brave and splendid. While I—oh, well, it is tiresome to talk about oneself. You'll come to see us as soon as you can. Mildred will be so anxious. And please, please be careful for her sake."

For half a moment Barbara had an impulse to mention Mildred Thornton's intimacy with Brooks Curtis, the young newspaper correspondent, to her brother. But then she realized that there was not time. Moreover, Mildred would probably prefer telling him whatever there might be to tell herself.

Besides, at this instant Nona Davis appeared, looking both worried and annoyed. What had become of Barbara Meade that she was not attending to her duties? Was she ill again?

Naturally on discovering Barbara talking to a stranger at such a time Nona was puzzled and displeased. She had never seen Dick Thornton to know him, although Mildred had of course frequently spoken of her brother.

A few seconds later, when the necessary explanations had been made, Nona and Barbara went together into the temporary hospital building. Dick found his quarters and dropped asleep. He had not thought it worth while to mention to Barbara that he had been working like a Hercules since earliest dawn.

CHAPTER XVIII
A Reappearance

After several weeks of the ambulance work, Barbara found herself growing more accustomed to it. Not that she had recovered from her horror and dread. But she had at least learned to control her nerves and to become more useful. She was able to make up her mind, as Dick had told her, that everybody felt much as she did, but simply showed greater stoicism.

Fortunately for Barbara, her first two weeks of work came after a lull in the fighting at NeuveChapelle. There were but few desperately wounded soldiers to be brought to the hospital. Most of the men were either ill from natural causes or from some disease contracted in the trenches. Only now and then an occasional shot from across the line found the way to its victim.

Then frequently during this period Barbara and Dick enjoyed opportunities for short conversations. Several times Dick had received leaves of absence to come and see his sister and her friends.

He was immediately a great favorite with the hospital staff. He and Nona Davis seemed to understand each other particularly well. There was some bond of likeness between them. Both of them moved slowly, had an air of languor and easy grace, and yet when the necessity arose were capable of the swiftest and most definite action.

Several times the idea came to Barbara: would Dick and Nona some day learn to care seriously for each other? She used to feel lonely and cold at this thought, yet all the while recognizing that this might prove a beautiful relationship.

Nona seemed so brave. The other girl could not but marvel.

Whatever work she had to do she went through it and so far as one could see showed no qualms or misgivings. In the dreary ride from the field Nona used always to take charge of the patient who suffered most. And though sometimes her delicate face was like alabaster she never faltered either in her care or cheerfulness.

Dr. Milton, a young Englishman who had charge of one of the new ambulances, was open in his praise of Nona's assistance. He could scarcely believe she had so little previous nursing experience. But then Daisy

Redmond insisted that the young surgeon was half in love with the southern girl and so his opinion was prejudiced.

Moreover, Mildred Thornton also seemed greatly cheered by her brother's appearance, although this was natural enough. At first she had been frightened for his safety, but as the days passed and no fresh fighting took place her fears abated.

By nature Mildred Thornton was extremely reticent. Never being congenial with her mother, she had never made a confidant of her. Then, while Dick always told her his secrets, she had but few of her own and not specially liking to talk, kept these to herself. So perhaps by accident and perhaps because of her nature she said little to her brother about her new acquaintances, Mrs. Curtis and Brooks Curtis. In a vague way Dick knew of them both, understood that Mildred now and then went to call on the mother and liked her. But he did not know that Mildred ever saw the young man or that she received frequent letters from him. Nor that these letters were brought to her in a mysterious fashion by Anton, the half-witted French boy, by an especial arrangement.

In the rear of the garden there chanced to be a loose stone in the old convent wall. The letters were thrust under this stone. So whenever Mildred was alone and had the chance she could collect her own mail.

There seemed nothing so specially remarkable to Mildred in this arrangement. The letters usually only contained a short note written to her. The rest of the enclosure were presumably the letters which Brooks Curtis was sending to his newspaper in the United States through Mildred's aid. For she used to address them to the street and number he had given her and mail them at the same time she mailed her own home letters.

Probably Mildred did not talk more of her friendship with the young newspaper man because she did not wish to betray what she was doing for him. There could be no harm in it and yet there was a possibility that the hospital authorities might object, everything was being so strictly and so carefully managed.

Only two or three times since their walk together had Mildred seen the young man himself. But she always spent the hours she was off duty with his mother and apparently knew the history of the son from his youth up.

Mrs. Curtis said that she herself was a New Yorker, but that her husband had been a foreigner, of what nationality she did not mention. But Brooks had been taught several languages when he was a young boy, both French and German. These were most useful to him in his work. Then she spoke freely of the admiration her son felt for Mildred and that ordinarily he did not like the society of girls.

So Mildred was pleased and a little flattered. Brooks Curtis was unusually clever, there was no disputing that, and at times had agreeable manners, only he was moody and changeable. Possibly had Mildred met him under other circumstances she would have felt no interest in him. But she had a kind of fellow feeling for her own countryman in a strange land.

And though Mildred was not aware of it, Mrs. Curtis was an adept in the art of flattery. No one in her life had ever said such charming things to the girl, or made her feel of so great importance. Mrs. Curtis hung on everything Mildred said. She persuaded her she could not have endured her own loneliness except for the girl's kindness.

Perhaps owing to the same streak of reticence and a little self-depreciation, Mildred had not yet become very intimate with the other three American Red Cross girls who were her companions. They were nice to her, but Barbara and Nona had developed a friendship which made her feel a little left out, and Eugenia was too cold and too occupied with her work for confidences. One so often wondered if she could be a real flesh-and-blood woman.

So the days passed. In spite of the tragedy surrounding them a kind of routine filled the lives of the Red Cross girls, as it did those of the soldiers at the front except during the hours of actual warfare.

Actually one afternoon Nona and Barbara drove back to the hospital in the ambulance with only one patient, who was fast asleep for most of the journey.

By and by Nona took a letter out of her pocket. "I have been meaning to tell you, Barbara, and have never had a real chance. Lady Dorian, the friend we met on the ship, has been acquitted of the charges against her in London. She says that they were not able to prove anything, though she does not feel sure that she is not still regarded with suspicion. The papers she carried with her were family papers and had nothing to do with political matters. She declares that she is not in the least a German sympathizer, but that she longs and prays for peace. She has been trying to establish some kind of peace party in London, I think. Some time ago, in the first letter I received from her, she told me to ask Eugenia if she still objected to our friendship, now that there were no clouds against her. Of course Eugenia said, 'No.' So Lady Dorian writes me that she is coming over to our hospital. Not to nurse; she does not know how to do that, but she has given the hospital a lot of money and is going to help with the office work. I am deeply interested to see her again. You know I had a feeling we would meet. I don't often take fancies to people, but I have taken a strange one to her."

Barbara nodded. "I like her too, but perhaps not just in the way you do. For I still feel there is some mystery about her that makes me uncomfortable. But she is beautiful and charming and I shall look forward to her coming."

That same afternoon just at dusk Barbara and Nona arrived at the Sacred Heart Hospital. They were so tired that they went straight to their rooms and laid down.

Half an hour afterwards Eugenia Peabody knocked at the door and opened it. She had with her a tall woman dressed quietly in a plain dark-blue dress fitting the lines of her figure closely. Even in the dusk she gave one a sense of beauty and poise, and there was an odor about her like lilacs.

She kissed both girls as if they had been real friends.

"I have been hearing of what you have been doing and I'm very proud of you," she murmured. "I hope I may be useful too."

But Nona half saw and half felt that the woman for whom she had conceived such an intense fancy looked very weary and sad.

CHAPTER XIX
The Test

O ne morning a short time afterwards, as the Red Cross ambulance drew within two miles of the field hospital, the chauffeur stopped.

For a quarter of an hour before, though no one had spoken of it, the four occupants of the wagon had heard the far-off echo of a tremendous cannonading. It was not possible to locate the sound.

Now the chauffeur turned to Dr. Milton.

"I don't know whether we ought to report for duty this morning," he volunteered. "I've an idea the trouble we hoped was pretty well over in this neighborhood has broken out again. We will probably get into the thick of things if we go much nearer."

Dr. Milton's lips tightened. "That's what we are here for, isn't it? Oh, I understand what you mean; of course you have no fear for yourself. Let's think the situation over."

The young fellow who had charge of the particular ambulance in which Nona and Barbara were acting as nurses was a young Englishman who had volunteered for the service from one of the Manchester automobile factories. He was a skilled and trained workman and believed that in guiding a Red Cross ambulance he was doing more for his country than in actual fighting. But he was as gallant as possible and utterly fearless for his own safety.

The two men were together on the front seat of the car. Nevertheless, when they began talking, as long as the ambulance was no longer in movement, both Barbara and Nona were able to understand the subject of their conversation.

However, neither girl spoke immediately.

Nona Davis turned to gaze at her companion.

But Barbara seemed to have her entire attention engaged in straining her ears to the noise of the bombarding. Now and again there was a faint lull and then the noise broke out with added fury. Sometimes the sound came from one side of the line and sometimes from the other. There could be no disputing the fact, fighting had indeed begun again.

Dr. Milton swung around and looked at Nona.

"Miss Davis," he began. "I know it is a great deal to ask of you and Miss Meade. We are several miles this side of the hospital and the walk will be a long one; nevertheless, won't you both attempt it? Of course, you have guessed, just as we have, that trouble has broken out afresh in our neighborhood and if our ambulance goes on much farther we may at any moment be in the midst of it. We are flying the Red Cross flag, but that does not always save us, and couldn't save us in any case from the bursting of a shell. Yet Martin and I feel we must go on toward the battlefield, as we are needed now more than any other time. We must not take you into such danger, so if you will leave us——"

Nona's golden brown eyes wore almost an exalted look, they were so free from thought of self.

"But won't nurses also be more needed?" she asked, although not requiring an answer to so self-evident a question.

"Dr. Milton, I entirely appreciate your feeling, but honestly I am not afraid. I don't exactly know why, but I don't believe anything will happen to me. If it does, why of course when one comes here for the Red Cross work, one expects to take chances." Again Nona glanced toward Barbara, who still had not spoken. "Do you think there would be any danger if Miss Meade should walk back to the hospital alone?" she asked.

Really Nona had not the least idea of the insult her words implied to the other girl. Not for worlds would she have wounded or offended her! Neither did she believe Barbara a coward because she felt that the work ahead of them might be too much for her. This business of nursing is often a matter of sensibility. The people with the finest nerves and tenderest hearts are least fitted for the profession. So it had become almost a matter of course in the past few weeks for the three American Red Cross girls to regard the fourth of their number in this light.

But Barbara flushed so painfully that tears filled her eyes.

"So that is what you think of me, is it, Nona?" she queried. But she offered no further reproaches; only turning quietly toward the driver of the ambulance said, "Drive on, will you, please. I too am unwilling to go back now. We will, of course, be as careful as possible, since only in that way can we really help."

Then nobody said another word for the next half an hour. Perhaps their hearts were too full for speech or their nerves on too terrible a tension. Also the noise of the firing as they approached nearer the line of the British trenches grew more appalling.

But along the way Nona slipped her hand inside Barbara's and though her lips were not opened, her apology was made and accepted. Moreover, in a sub-conscious fashion Barbara appreciated that no distrust had been intended. For indeed, the two girls were daily becoming closer and closer friends now that their ambulance work gave them the chance for spending long hours in each other's society. Unlike as they were they appreciated the very differences between them.

But now was not the time for thinking of themselves nor of their friendship.

The thought of what lay before them called only for brave silences.

With great skill and care the driver of their Red Cross ambulance moved in the direction of the battle. There could be no doubt in any mind of what was taking place. Therefore to approach even within the neighborhood of the little field hospital near the trenches required infinite caution and judgment.

Once the car stopped short. Thirty yards before them a giant shell tore through the air and fell, ripping a tunnel in the green earth. The big ambulance wagon felt the shock of the explosion, but was not sufficiently near to be endangered, except of course the thought would force itself: Next time would they escape so easily?

Yet mysteriously Nona and not even Barbara were so frightened as one might expect. In moments of great peril, as we all know, a courage is born which one does not have in the lesser moments of life.

Once Barbara thought with a whimsical twisting of her lips no one saw, that in all probability she was so terrified that she had no ordinary method of showing it. One could not scream or cry out and certainly one could not weep like a nervous school girl. Having made up her mind to go through with whatever lay before them, stoicism was the only possible way of facing the situation.

Finally the ambulance arrived at the edge of a woods about half a mile back from the stable which had been transformed into the temporary Red Cross hospital at the beginning of the fighting at NeuveChapelle.

For the moment the noise of the cannon and guns from the two lines of trenches lying so tragically near one another, made speech between the occupants of the wagon almost impossible. Yet the young Englishman brought his ambulance to a stand-still behind a clump of trees that so far had been spared from destruction.

"We must leave the ambulance here," he directed, "it will be wiser to bring the soldiers to the car, than run the risk of having it made a target."

The ambulance surgeon nodded; there was no time for discussion.

"Will you wait here or come with us nearer the hospital?" he asked, looking at Nona.

She made no reply, only started to follow the two men across the open field that lay between the hiding place of the ambulance and the work before them. Barbara silently kept at her side.

The girls could see the ground shake as if stirred by an earthquake. Then from the line, where they knew the British trenches to be concealed, poured a steady stream of low-lying smoke crawling across the land like innumerable serpents. This was returned in the same fashion, while overhead thundered the larger field guns, whose smoke hung like a giant cloud overhead.

None of the guns were being turned upon the open space over which the two girls and two men were running at a steady pace. Moreover, they were somewhat protected by the breastworks which had been thrown up before the little emergency hospital and the fact that the Red Cross flag flew from a tall flagstaff set in front of it, visible many miles away.

They were well in sight of the hospital when Barbara's former terror reasserted itself. With this first glimpse, things were worse than her most terrified dreams had pictured.

Running across the meadows whenever a lull came in the firing were soldiers bearing their stricken comrades. Because few of them dared cease from their own labor of firing, the men at the work of rescue were not soldiers but those who had specially volunteered for the saving of the wounded.

It is not worth while to speak of the scene at the field hospital. If one's own imagination cannot picture it, perhaps it is better never to know of the horrors of a battlefield.

For the next few hours Barbara and Nona worked as never before in their lives. They became inspired human machines. No longer did they consciously hear even the noises of the cannonading. Every instant something had to be done. There were wounds to be cleansed, bandages put on. The surgeons assisted when an operation could not be delayed.

Often the two American Red Cross girls stood close together without recognizing each other's presence.

Once and only once did Barbara Meade wake up.

By chance she was standing by the opening of a great tent that had been put up near the stable now serving as a temporary relief station after it had become too crowded for usefulness.

Some special sight or sound must have attracted her attention, although she was not aware of it at the time. Her hands were busy holding a basin of water, but her eyes were drawn in another direction. At that moment Dick Thornton came into the tent bearing a wounded man in his arms.

Barbara paid no attention to the soldier. She found herself wondering two things: one of them why she had not thought before of Dick's peril, and the other, how had she been able to recognize him so swiftly when it was scarcely possible to see his face?

Surely the Dick she recalled lounging in the beautiful old New York library smoking a cigarette, wearing a velvet coat, perfumed and smiling, had indeed vanished. This fellow's face was covered with smoke and blood, his khaki coat had been wrapped about a comrade so that now he was in his shirt sleeves, but the shirt was torn and crimson.

Was Dick wounded? Barbara had no chance to ask. Her friend did not look toward her—was apparently not aware of her presence. A surgeon had come forward to assist him, and finding an empty cot he put his burden down upon it. The next instant he had gone.

To Barbara's credit she did not let the basin in her hands tremble for even the slightest instant, neither did she falter in body or spirit. She closed her lips tight together, stiffened her body and went on with her work.

But when her task was finished perhaps she showed the passing of an unusual strain. Anyhow the doctor whom she had been helping chanced to glance at her.

"I say, Miss Meade," he said kindly, "you are overdoing things. Nothing to be gained by that. Go out in the fresh air, get away from this if you can and rest ten or fifteen minutes. You should know when you feel better."

The girl hesitated.

"Do as I tell you," the surgeon continued more sternly. "We haven't time to have you on our hands, and you look like you might keel over after a little more of this."

Then wearily Barbara crept out into the fresh air, feeling all of a sudden that her knees did not belong to her and that she was nearly unable to stand.

But once outside and with no duty before her, she managed to walk for some little distance. In truth she did long to escape for a while from the sorrow about her. But of course at such a time and in such a place this was impossible. Between her and the battleground were only a few meadows and fields. Nevertheless, the girl sank thankfully down upon the earth, closing her eyes. At least she need *see* no more terrors of battle for a little time.

How long she kept her eyes closed Barbara did not know, but when she opened them she stared ahead of her with nothing definite in her mind, as she was too fatigued to think.

What she saw, however, was a small field ambulance waving a Red Cross flag tearing across a space at no great distance away from her. It traveled so fast that the car shook from its own vibrations, and in the chauffeur's seat Barbara had an instantaneous vision of the same stained face she had recognized a short while before.

It was all plain enough, Dick Thornton was engaged in the work of rescue. He must have driven his field ambulance back into the danger line and be again returning with wounded men.

Barbara got quickly on her feet. Some instinct drove her forward, or was it the inspiration of that careening wagon with its load of human freight?

Dick must have had a forewarning of danger, for never had he attempted reaching safety with a more reckless effort at speed. Yet the disaster came when he had about ceased to look for it. They were nearing the hospital, there were no guns trained in their direction. Yet possibly a mistake was made somewhere at this moment. The German gunners may have thought that they had located a position where British officers were giving their commands.

Unexpectedly, and of course without warning, Barbara saw a cloud of smoke surrounding the field ambulance, heard the noise of an exploding shell and before the car overturned, Dick Thornton, with his arms outspread, pitch forward and land with his face and half his body buried in the earth.

Nor did the firing cease in the place where he lay.

CHAPTER XX
A Girl's Deed

I t may be just as well that there are crises in human life when one acts without thinking.

So it was now with Barbara Meade. She did not consider her own danger, nor perhaps the foolishness of her deed. All she saw was that Dick Thornton was lying defenseless upon the ground with a rain of shrapnel descending about him.

It may have been that he was dead and that nothing could further injure or aid him, but Barbara did not contemplate this. She did not cry for help nor even turn back for a moment toward the hospital. Quick as a flash, with the swift movement and decision characteristic of the girl, she darted from her own place of comparative safety out into the open field.

The ambulance had overturned slowly so that one-half of it had sunk down at the side, but in any case the wounded men were safer within its covered walls than under the angry skies.

It required only a few moments for the girl to reach the prostrate figure of the American boy. He had not stirred after his fall, so that Barbara instantly dropped down on her knees beside him and with a nurse's knowledge took hold of the limp hand that was lying in the dust, to count the beating of his pulse. It was so faint she could hardly be sure of it.

She must find out his injury, and yet first he must be gotten to a place of greater security.

Curious that Barbara, who had been so fearful of the horrors of war, should be so fearless now! But it did not occur to her that she was in equal peril there by the body of her wounded friend. The gun fire which might again strike him was equally apt to choose her for a victim.

Indeed, the girl's body partly covered that of the boy as she leaned over him and seizing him firmly by the shoulders began dragging him backwards.

If they could get behind the partly overturned ambulance perhaps in a little while the firing might cease in their neighborhood long enough for the hospital staff to rescue them.

Barbara set her teeth. If she had been weary a short while before she had forgotten it now. But Dick was tall and heavy and she was so stupidly, ridiculously small. However, Barbara made no effort to be gentle. If Dick had been a log of wood that she had been forced to bring to a certain spot she would have hauled it in much the same way.

Yet once she believed she heard Dick groan and this was perhaps her one consciously glad moment, for at least he was alive; before she had not been altogether sure.

But once behind the wagon, Barbara sat down and drew Dick's head into her lap. Gently she pushed the hair back from his face and then from a little canteen she always carried poured a few drops of water between his lips. He seemed to swallow them. She could see now that his right shoulder had been struck and that his arm hung strangely at his side. There might be other worse injuries, of course, but this one she could discern.

Then Barbara wiped the grime from her companion's face with the white linen cloths she had in her pocket. Only then did the tears start to her eyes, because the blood which had been stopped by the dirt encrusting it began to flow afresh. Dick also had a wound across his face. It did not appear serious, but Barbara had suddenly thought of Mrs. Thornton's pride in Dick's appearance and of what she would suffer should she see him like this. The girl had a sudden, unreasonable feeling of resentment against Dick himself. After all, what right had he to risk his life in this horrible war? He was an American and owed no duty to another country.

The next instant Barbara realized her own absurdity. Was she not in her way doing just what Dick had done, only of course far less nobly and well? And after all, were not men and women fighting for the right, brothers and sisters in the divinest sense?

When Dick Thornton finally opened his eyes Barbara was crying in earnest. It was ridiculous and utterly undignified of her. Here she had done the bravest kind of deed quickly and efficiently, but now that she should be showing all the calmness of a well-regulated trained nurse, she had taken to weeping.

Of course, Dick did not return at once to a full understanding of the situation. For to Barbara's credit it must be said that while she was indulging in tears she was also bandaging Dick's forehead with all possible skill. It was perhaps the touch of her hands that had awakened him.

For a moment he gazed at the girl stupidly. But when her work was finished and his head again rested quietly in her lap, Dick endeavored to look about him. A movement made him faint with pain, yet he could turn his eyes without stirring. Vaguely he saw the overturned ambulance in front of them, heard faint moans on the inside. Then there was the field. He recalled driving like mad across it and the explosion that had plunged him out of the car. What had taken place was becoming fairly clear except for the presence of his little western friend. What on earth was Barbara Meade doing here in a desperately dangerous situation? He remembered now having seen her assisting one of the surgeons inside the hospital tent earlier in the day. At least he believed he had seen her; there had been no moment then even for thought.

But what must he do now?

"Barbara," Dick began with surprising firmness, "you must get out of this death trap at once. The Lord only knows how you got here! Some one will look after us as soon as there is half a chance."

But Dick's last words were lost. Over in the dust a few feet from the place where he had first fallen a piece of broken shell fell with a kind of shriek. Stone and earth shot up in the air like a geyser and falling again partly covered the young man and Barbara and also the white sides of the ambulance.

"Don't talk, Dick," Barbara returned firmly. "You are right, some one will look after us as soon as possible."

Perhaps another five minutes passed, perhaps half an hour; there is no way of counting time in danger. Now and then a bullet or a piece of shrapnel passed beyond them or sunk into the earth at no great distance away. Dick again lost consciousness, Barbara remained almost equally still. Whatever fate might send they must accept.

But while Barbara Meade had given no thought to the nearness of the relief hospital and the men and women at work there, when she had made her swift rush to Dick Thornton's aid, naturally the overturning of the Red Cross ambulance had not gone long unobserved.

As everyone except Barbara was at work at the moment of the actual accident to the car, no one had seen her immediate action. However, the noise of the explosions so close to them naturally attracted the attention of the hospital staff. It was unusual, although it did happen now and then, for the German firing to be directed toward a Red Cross hospital. Perhaps it was intentional, perhaps a mistake had been made; one could only accept the fact that war is war.

Through a small telescope one of the hospital surgeons studied the position of the overturned ambulance a short time after Barbara succeeded in drawing Dick behind its shelter. Then he became aware that one of their

Red Cross nurses was also beside the ambulance. He could distinctly see her uniform, even the Red Cross on her arm.

The next moment he called Dr. Milton, who happened to be passing with Nona Davis on their way to another case.

You may remember that the accident had taken place between a quarter and a half mile across the fields.

Therefore it was not difficult when Nona's turn came to look through the telescope to recognize Barbara Meade. Dick she did not recognize, but indeed she paid scant attention to the khaki figure on the ground. Her interest was in her friend.

As soon as possible six volunteers made their way to the ambulance. Dick was carried safely back to the hospital and the two wounded men inside the ambulance whom he had been trying to save. Barbara walked beside them.

A little later, when the firing in the neighborhood had entirely ceased, the ambulance itself was righted and dragged back to the hospital for repairs. Fortunately, the car itself had been little injured.

CHAPTER XXI
An Unexpected Situation

Dick Thornton for a short time was desperately ill.

He had, of course, been removed to the Sacred Heart Hospital as soon as possible in order that his sister Mildred might be near him. But both Mildred and Barbara helped with the nursing.

It was considered wiser by the hospital authorities that Barbara should not return immediately to her work with the Red Cross ambulance at the front. She was more shaken by her experience than she herself realized, or at least so her appearance suggested. No one, not even Mildred Thornton, dreamed that a part of her pallor might be due to anxiety for Dick. Nevertheless, Barbara went about her work at the hospital looking spent and exhausted, yet she no longer flinched at anything she was called upon to do. The greater tragedies she had lately seen had taught her more self-control.

Just at first Barbara was not aware of the change in the attitude of the hospital staff toward her after her rescue of Dick Thornton. It had seemed such a natural action to her she had not given it any thought.

But Nona Davis had not seen it in the same light, nor had Dr. Milton nor the other nurses and physicians near the battlefield.

Everywhere there was talk of the valor and common sense of the young American girl. Whether or not it was true, she was given the credit for having saved Dick's life. Had he remained unprotected a stray shot must have done for him.

Mildred made no effort to conceal her gratitude and affection for Barbara, and even Lady Dorothy Mathers and Daisy Redmond, the two English girls who at first had small faith in Barbara's ability, were now generously kind to her. Actually Lady Dorothy apologized for having previously slighted her, while Alexina McIntyre gathered Barbara into her capable arms.

"You're a wee thing, there is no denying it, but I've always believed you had grit and now you have proved it."

So in course of time Barbara grew happier and stronger, though not, as it turned out, until Dick was out of danger. The wound on his face healed rapidly enough, but the trouble had been with his splintered shoulder. He would hardly be useful at the front for some time to come.

Nevertheless, though Barbara remained behind for the regular staff nursing, Nona Davis continued in the ambulance service. The suggestion was made that she be relieved by one of the other nurses, but Nona preferred to make no change. For some reason she seemed peculiarly fitted for the work at the front. It required a coolness and obedience to orders that she was able to give. Her lack of long training did not count so seriously against her, since she was always under a surgeon's orders. Moreover, her courage and devotion never appeared to falter.

Often when she returned to the hospital at night Eugenia Peabody would look at her in amazement. Could Nona be made of flesh and blood? She seemed so slender and fragile and yet was like fine steel. The truth was that all her life Nona had been accustomed to taking care of some one, so that she thought far less of herself and her own sensations than other girls of her age. Moreover, back of her stretched a long line of cavalier ancestors, who have a peculiar quality of endurance under conditions of war, whatever their weakness in times of peace.

But really Nona was animated by none of these toploftical ideas; she was merely doing the best she could in the place where she seemed most needed.

However, other persons besides Eugenia marveled at her. Now and then when they were both free, Lady Dorian and Nona spent an hour or so together. The older woman was assisting with the business affairs of the hospital. An outsider can scarcely realize how much business there is that must be wisely administered. So Lady Dorian spent her time ordering supplies and watching over their disposal, but she made no friends except with Nona. An air of mystery still clung like a tangible atmosphere about her, and though the rest of the hospital staff were aware of it and did not understand her presence among them, they were too busy to give her much attention or thought.

Yet Nona Davis frequently thought of her in her long journeys back and forth. In spite of their increasing intimacy Lady Dorian had told her nothing more of herself. She mentioned no details of her arrest in London nor of the reasons the authorities had for finally releasing her. So Nona could not help feeling a slight curiosity, although she tried to smother it by scolding herself for her lack of good taste. Certainly one should never wish to know anything of a friend's life except what the friend wishes to tell, and yet at times it is hard not to desire the knowledge.

However, Nona's own affairs at this period should have been sufficiently absorbing to have made her forget other people's. The soldiers she had helped to care for, the surgeons she was in the habit of assisting, showed a peculiar affection and kindness for the young southern girl. And Dr. Milton made no effort to disguise his devotion.

At first when he discovered his own emotion the young English physician had no intention of betraying himself. He had come to the war to do his duty and not to give way to the ridiculous weakness of falling in love. But Nona had proved too much for him. So far, however, he had sufficient self-control not to have spoken of it to her. And if he showed his feeling in other ways Nona gave no sign of having understood, so the young surgeon had not been able to decide whether she felt more than a passing friendliness for him.

Nevertheless, he was glad one morning to be entrusted with a special message which was to be given in person to Miss Nona Davis.

An orderly had called at the temporary hospital near the British line of trenches to say that Colonel Dalton would like to speak to Miss Davis at his headquarters.

Naturally Nona was surprised by the message. She knew, of course, that after his recovery Colonel Dalton had returned to his command. There was almost daily talk of him, as he was regarded as one of the most capable officers at the front. But she had not seen him since the hour of their conversation by his bedside. What could he possibly wish of her? However, the interview was to take place a little before noon on the same day and an officer would call to escort her into the presence of his superior.

Frankly other persons beside the girl were mystified by Colonel Dalton's command. He was not in the habit of paying any attention to the Red Cross work or its workers. His reputation was that of a stern disciplinarian, whom his men respected but did not always like. So when Dr. Milton suggested that his intention might be to bestow some mark of favor upon Miss Davis for her devotion to the soldiers, no one took the idea seriously. Fortunately Nona did not even hear of it.

Before noon, however, she was ready to do as she had been bidden. She was waiting in the rear of the relief hospital when a young officer in the uniform of a lieutenant of the South Lancastershire regiment, riding one horse and leading another, drew up before her and dismounted.

Almost without regarding him Nona allowed him to help her into the saddle. Then they set off across country together, the young lieutenant a little in the lead. The secret of an officer's headquarters is sometimes so carefully guarded that not even his own soldiers know its exact location.

Nona was not even particularly interested. She realized that she rode about three-quarters of a mile and then stopped in front of what appeared like an immense pile of brushwood. Behind it was a small wooden building, evidently a temporary structure, and inside the building, seated before a small pine table with a telephone receiver in his hand, was Colonel Dalton.

Here at last Nona became vitally interested. She had been told that innumerable telephone wires, most of them underground, connected the British officer's quarters with the trenches at the front as well as with the headquarters of other officers and with the different positions of the field artillery. Here was certain proof of it. The officers with the men in the trenches must take their commands from their superiors who were in truth the "gods behind the machines."

The lieutenant saluted. Colonel Dalton returned the salute curtly. Nona simply waited and watched.

By and by Colonel Dalton put down the telephone receiver.

"Be seated," he said briefly, and Nona sat down on a wooden stool the younger officer thrust toward her. She had no special sensation of awe; she was seldom afraid of people except in social life. This was simply a part of her day's work. Nevertheless she wondered why Colonel Dalton was frowning at her so severely.

The same instant he took a bundle of papers from inside his pocket.

"Sorry to trouble you with this, Miss Davis, but for the present you seem the best person to get hold of. I remember our talk at the hospital, and moreover, I've the impression you can answer questions and keep your own counsel when it's necessary. There is some ugly work going on at the Sacred Heart Hospital. I've reason to believe that there is a spy among the workers over there. Is there any one you can think of who might be willing to give news of the British positions, the amount of our ammunition and other facts to the enemy? Think this over quietly and coolly. I promise you that no one will be held responsible whose guilt is not plainly proved and also that whatever you are willing to tell me will be kept in strictest confidence."

"But why do you think such a thing? How can you possibly imagine?" Nona faltered, and then appreciated that this was not the manner in which to address an officer. Colonel Dalton would not make such an accusation without due proof of his suspicion.

Nona had a dreadful sensation of horror and confusion. Surely Colonel Dalton must be mistaken. Never were there a more devoted, more sincere group of workers than the Red Cross nurses and physicians at the Sacred Heart Hospital. That treason could dwell among them was out of the question. Yet all the while the American girl was voicing this silent protest in her own heart, automatically she was reviewing the name and character of every member of their staff. There was no one, no one, who could not be wholly trusted, whose family and whose history were not open books.

Then a face and figure passed before the girl's vision and in a flash she controlled the leaping of the hot blood to her cheeks.

Nona looked directly at Colonel Dalton.

"You have asked me a question I will not answer," she returned quietly. "I do not, of course, know whether you have the right to force me, but I feel that I have no right to say a single word that would reflect on any man or woman at our hospital. What I could tell you would amount to nothing; it would only be guessing at best. For I have no actual reason for being suspicious of any one."

"No *actual* reason?" Colonel Dalton repeated. "Have you any reason at all?"

"No," Nona returned.

The Colonel glanced again at the papers in his hands. "Because you were so kind as to nurse me at the Sacred Heart Hospital and because I am aware of the noble work their nurses and doctors have been doing for the wounded, I want no evil gossip to surround you. Do not mention my errand, but say to your superintendent that I will call in person to see her tomorrow evening. Perhaps you are right in not betraying whomever it is you seem to suspect. Good-by."

Colonel Dalton again bowed his head, and as another officer had entered the room to speak to him, Nona hurried out.

The same lieutenant escorted her back to her starting point, but once again Nona paid no attention to him. She was in a tumult of surprise, apprehension and sorrow. A spy at the Sacred Heart Hospital, what knowledge had Colonel Dalton to go upon? Yet he appeared convinced and was too wise a man to accept a suspicion without proof.

No intimate personal sorrow had ever disturbed Nona Davis more seriously. Yet these were days when one could not give way. She must continue with her work as if nothing had happened and Colonel Dalton had commanded that she confide in no one. Yet if she could only speak of his suspicion to one single person, perhaps her own fears might be dissipated, or else, or else—here Nona scarcely faced her own thought. Perhaps the telling might enable the offender to escape while there was still opportunity.

She was dazed and sick when her escort assisted her to alight for the second time. Yet she had a vague sensation that his eyes were gazing at her with a strange combination of amusement and sympathy. But of course she must have been dreaming, because after she had walked several yards away she thought she overheard him say, "Are you the gardener's son?" And really she had no right to believe the young officer had suddenly lost his mind.

CHAPTER XXII
Recognition

N ona Davis delivered Colonel Dalton's message to the superintendent of the Sacred Heart Hospital. However, after second thought Colonel Dalton also sent a letter explaining the circumstances more fully and asking for a private meeting in order that a thorough investigation be made.

A woman of about forty with a large experience of life, Miss Grey, though deeply disturbed by the British officer's suspicion, did not allow herself to go to pieces over it. She knew that they were living in the heat and turmoil of the most terrible war in history, where every day thousands of men and women were willing to give their lives to afford the slightest aid to their country. Everywhere there had been stories of spies and oftentimes many of them were the last persons to be suspected. It was dreadful to learn that a spy had crept within the shelter of the Sacred Heart Hospital, and yet there was no reason why one place should be spared more than another.

So very quietly Miss Grey set to work to study possibilities for herself, in order that she might be able later to assist Colonel Dalton in his effort to unearth the guilty person. She knew the name and something of the past history of every individual on her hospital staff, including both the outside and inside servants. This, owing to the conditions of war, she had considered a part of her duty. Indeed, she kept a small book in which their names, previous addresses and occupations were carefully registered and the Red Cross nurses had also presented their nursing certificates with a brief outline of their circumstances.

So without discussing the situation with any one else seriously, Miss Grey studied the contents of this little volume, intending to hand it to Colonel Dalton as soon as they met.

Without the least sense of prejudice she found herself most interested in the latest arrivals at the hospital. Of course, there was as yet no reason, so far as she knew, why one person should be suspected beyond another. The spy may have been in their midst many months waiting the opportunity for betrayal. Nevertheless, as the discovery of treachery was so recent, it was natural for her to guess that the evildoer was a comparatively new member of their staff.

The newcomers chanced to be the eight new nurses, four of them American and four British, who had begun work about two months before, and Lady Dorian, who was the last arrival.

Just as Nona had felt a sudden chill at the thought of Lady Dorian's painful experience and her evident wish not to talk of herself, so Miss Grey frowned and flushed when she came upon her name in the hospital biography.

Had the authorities been wise in accepting Lady Dorian's presence among them and the very generous gifts she had made so soon after her trial in London? It was true that nothing had then been proven against her and so very probably she had naught to do with the attempted destruction of the ship upon which she had chanced to be a passenger. However, it might have been the better part of valor to have regarded Lady Dorian with possible scepticism, more especially as so little was known of her previous history.

Yet with no facts at her disposal Miss Grey took the only wise course, she reserved judgment.

Thirty-six hours later, just after dusk, Colonel Dalton, accompanied by the lieutenant who was one of his aides, rode up to the Sacred Heart Hospital. He went straight into the business office of the superintendent, where he spent half an hour with Miss Grey, Mrs. Payne and other persons in positions of trust.

At the close of that time a command was issued, asking the surgeons, nurses and servants in relays of eight or ten to come into the office in order that Colonel Dalton might question them. No one, of course, except Nona Davis, had any conception of why a British officer should be devoting his valuable time to interviewing the members of a hospital staff for any purpose whatsoever.

But by chance Eugenia, Mildred, Barbara and Nona, Lady Mathers, Alexina McIntyre and Lady Dorian made one of the latest groups. It was not by chance, however, that Nona went first to Lady Dorian's tiny room at the top of the tallest tower and asked that they might go downstairs together.

To the girl's horror Lady Dorian absolutely refused to accompany her.

She was sitting by a window with only a lighted taper in the room, apparently nervous and unhappy.

"Please present my respects to Commander Dalton," she said, "and say that as I am not well it will be impossible for me to see him." Lady Dorian spoke so quietly, as if there were no question of her wish not being respected, that Nona was frightened.

"But you *must* come, please," the younger girl urged. "I am afraid you don't realize how important it is that all of us be present. Don't you appreciate that whatever reason Colonel Dalton may have for talking with us, it would not look well for any one of us to refuse to be interviewed?"

But Nona's arguments and persuasions proved of no avail. Finally she had to go down to the office with the others, leaving Lady Dorian in her own room.

Nevertheless Nona did not dare repeat aloud the message her friend had given her. She only whispered its substance confusedly in Miss Grey's ear and the next moment the superintendent left the room.

No one of the four American Red Cross girls nor any one else present ever forgot the next quarter of an hour.

Colonel Dalton was intensely angry. He considered that he was not doing the work of a soldier and only his interest in the Sacred Heart Hospital induced him to conduct an inquiry of such a nature. However, the traitor had to be discovered and at once.

In his hand he held the bunch of papers which Nona recognized as the same he had in his conversation with her. Also she recognized the lieutenant as the young officer who had previously escorted her and who had made such an extraordinary speech at their moment of parting.

However, Colonel Dalton was only beginning his cross-examination of the latest comers when the door of the office again opened and Miss Grey entered accompanied by Lady Dorian.

Nona gave a little gasp of relief and dismay. For never had she seen any one look so ill and wretched as Lady Dorian. She was plainly making every effort to keep her face averted from the gaze of the older man, who was sitting in a chair beside a small table.

But Nona was the more amazed when she turned to see what impression had been made upon Colonel Dalton. Disturbed by the opening of the door, he had glanced up. Now his face was no longer crimson from anger and outdoor exposure, but white and drawn, and his eyes expressed extraordinary surprise and discomfort.

For a moment his lips moved without making a sound, but the next he had assumed his former military bearing.

"In the past few weeks letters have been mailed from this hospital, supposedly addressed to a newspaper in New York City for publication, but in reality exposing the secrets of the British army in this neighborhood to our enemy," he began. "It should not be difficult for some one on this staff to tell me who posted these letters and where the information they contain was obtained." The officer then struck the table harshly with the papers in his hand. "One of these letters got through the post, the others are in my possession, so there will be little chance for the informant to escape. Has any one a suggestion as to who the man or woman may be?"

At the question had all the persons in the room been spies they could scarcely have appeared more miserable and guilty. Moreover, for a moment no one attempted to reply.

Presently Mildred Thornton walked over to the table.

Mildred was not handsome, yet at this moment her dignity, her refinement and more than that, her look of intelligence which was like her distinguished father's, had never been more apparent.

"Will you show me the letters you speak of, Colonel Dalton?" she asked in a low tone.

The officer appeared to hesitate, but after a careful study of the girl he gave the letters into her hands.

Near them was a lamp on the table and Mildred stooped as she went rapidly through the papers. Then she straightened up and her lips were like chalk.

"I mailed the letters," she said distinctly. "But listen to me for a moment while I explain, then I'm ready to take whatever punishment I deserve."

There was a complete silence. Mildred spoke very calmly, very proudly; nevertheless, no one of her three American friends believed her. Mildred's statement was so incredible, she must have lost her senses. Instinctively Barbara started forward to protest, but both Eugenia and Nona held on to her.

"Wait until she has spoken," Eugenia ordered.

Colonel Dalton himself did not appear particularly convinced. A spy was not apt to proclaim guilt with so little pressure. Yet the young woman looked as if she had brains.

"A young man and his mother have been staying in this neighborhood almost ever since our arrival," Mildred began. "Brooks Curtis, the man called himself. We met him on board the steamer coming over to England

and he told me that he was a newspaper correspondent and meant to report the war. I don't know anything else about him, but I liked him, although my friends did not." Here Mildred flushed and her hands trembled, yet she went on bravely. "Mrs. Curtis settled in the neighborhood in one of the peasants' cottages and I used to see her nearly every week and now and then her son. One day Mr. Curtis told me he was having difficulty in mailing his letters to his New York paper and asked me to mail them for him. Also he asked me not to mention the fact. I was very stupid, I was worse than stupid, but of course I did not dream of what I was really doing. Still, I feel that I deserve imprisonment or punishment of some kind. I came to Europe to try to be of service to the soldiers and I've brought them misfortune." The girl for the moment could say nothing more. But then everybody in the room was equally aghast, Mildred's explanation was so astounding and at the same time so simple.

"Is there a way of getting hold of this young man to find out if your story is true?" Colonel Dalton demanded.

And this time Nona and Barbara answered together. "Mrs. Curtis could be found at the home of Mère Marie and Anton. From her one might obtain information concerning her son."

A moment later the two girls and the lieutenant were on their way to the hut of Mère Marie. A little later they returned with the news that Mrs. Curtis had disappeared the day before and the old peasant woman had no knowledge of her whereabouts.

But during their absence Colonel Dalton and Mildred had a long talk together, so the girl herself was able to convince him. He was very severe, he could find little excuse for her foolishness; nevertheless, recognizing at the end Mildred's innocence and utter inexperience of life, he assured her that she need fear no penalty. The British Government, however, would seek to find the young man calling himself Brooks Curtis, and on his arrest she would be expected to appear.

Finally Mildred was allowed to go up to her room and Barbara and Eugenia went with her. Lady Mathers and Alexina wandered off to express their opinions on the situation.

So by accident Nona Davis was left for a moment standing in the hall with the young English lieutenant. She had seen him several times lately, it was true, and yet she was annoyed at this moment to find him smiling at her in a surprisingly friendly fashion.

From the single rose bush in front of Mère Marie's cottage even in the darkness he had plucked a rose. Now he extended the rose to Nona.

"Have all Americans poor memories?" he asked. "Or is it because you wish to forget? Once upon a time there was a young man asleep in an English garden and lifting his eyes he saw a fairy princess standing over him with a rose in her dress as yellow as her hair."

Nona blushed delightfully. "You mean," she said, "that you are the gardener's son? Then you are well and back at your post again? I'm so glad."

Her companion nodded. "I am a son of Adam."

But at this moment Colonel Dalton, Miss Grey and Lady Dorian made their appearance and the young officer turned to salute his superior.

Miss Grey accompanied them to the door, leaving Nona and Lady Dorian alone.

Impulsively the younger girl kissed her friend. "I am so happy," she whispered.

Lady Dorian walked away with her. "I understand, dear," she returned. "The truth is Colonel Dalton and I knew each other very intimately in the past and I felt it might be pleasanter for us not to meet again. Naturally I did not dream of the seriousness of his errand. Some day I may tell you the whole story; now good night."

Nona went on upstairs without replying and the next hour the three girls devoted to trying to console Mildred Thornton.

It was Barbara's conviction that they would some day meet Brooks Curtis again. Then Mildred could repay his deceit by surrendering him to the British authorities. But Mildred had no wish to find the young man. If only he did no further harm to the Allies she wished that she might never see or hear of him again.

And the girls did not hear. Several months passed by and each day found them more and more absorbed in their Red Cross work.

Nona Davis did not mention Lady Dorian's confidence. However, there was little she *could* tell. The older woman had simply explained that she had spent several years in England, where she and Colonel Dalton had known each other intimately.

But there was too much for the Red Cross Girls to do, they were living too full lives themselves to give more than passing thoughts to other persons.

When Dick Thornton had in a measure recovered he returned to London.

So the early part of the winter vanished. Now and then there came a lull in the fighting between the armies of northern France. Afterwards it would break out again with greater violence.

Finally the climax came.

By chance Nona and Barbara, who had again joined the ambulance corps, first brought the news to the Sacred Heart Hospital. The order had come from Colonel Dalton. Later it was delivered in person by Lieutenant Hume.

The Sacred Heart Hospital must be abandoned. Having forced the British line for several miles, the Germans were now dangerously near. If the hospital wished to protect its wounded, to save supplies, to safeguard its workers, their present habitation must be abandoned.

No army ever moved its encampment with greater efficiency. In between their periods of nursing the four American girls assisted with the packing. No one of them ever forgot the experience. Yet at the last there was a sudden rush. The enemy was reported advancing before another refuge could be found for the Sacred Heart staff. Wounded soldiers had to be transported in half a dozen directions wherever a spot could be found for them. At the time there was no place for so many extra nurses.

It was Eugenia Peabody who finally made the suggestion to Miss Grey. She proposed that she and her three friends should find a retreat for themselves, and there await orders. It would relieve so much of the Superintendent's responsibility.

So one afternoon the four American girls were hurried away in one of the army motors to the nearest railroad station in a zone of safety.

The next morning, in a little less than a year after their arrival in Europe, they found themselves in a small French city.

A few days after Nona Davis suggested that they offer their services to the French Red Cross. Having come abroad to serve the Allies, it was natural they should wish to care for the wounded soldiers of the different nationalities.

This first volume in the American Red Cross series can, of course, only begin to tell the adventures and experiences of the four American girls, who, forgetful of self, offered their services to the wounded soldiers in the war. The stories of their lives and the friends they gather around them will be continued in the next book in the series, to be known as "The Red Cross Girls on the French Firing Line."

CPSIA information can be obtained
at www.ICGtesting.com
Printed in the USA
BVHW040941150822
644604BV00010B/315